HIDDEN DEVOTION
TRINITY MASTERS: SECRETS AND SINS
BOOK ONE

MARI CARR
LILA DUBOIS

Copyright 2017 by Mari Carr and Lila Dubois

All Rights Reserved.

No part of this book, with the exception of brief quotations for book reviews or critical articles, may be reproduced or transmitted in any form or by any means, electronic or mechanical, including photocopying, recording, or by any information storage and retrieval system without express written permission from the author.

This is a work of fiction. Names, characters, places, and incidents are the product of the author's imagination or are used fictitiously, and any resemblance to actual persons, living or dead, business establishments, events, or locales is entirely coincidental.

Editor: Kelli Collins

Cover artist: Lila Dubois

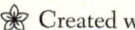 Created with Vellum

TRIGGER WARNINGS

The Trinity Masters series is a romantic suspense and all books contain explicit sex and depictions of violence (action scenes).

HIDDEN DEVOTION

Can an arranged marriage survive a broken heart...and a lifetime of lies?

She fell in love with her fiance. Normally that wouldn't be a problem, but Juliette Adams didn't pick Devon Asher. She's been engaged to him since she was a child–a modern day betrothal that she thought was wildly romantic.

Until Devon broke her heart.

If her life was normal, Juliette could end the engagement. But as a legacy member of America's oldest and most powerful secret society, Juliette is destined for a trinity marriage arranged by the society's secretive leader–the Grand Master–who just happens to be Juliette's brother.

When Juliette unexpectedly becomes leader of the Trinity Masters she has the power to finally end her engagement to Devon. And the power to recruit people like the geeky and sexy Franco Garcia Santiago.

But Devon isn't going to let her go without a fight, and

Franco uncovers dangerous secrets that could threaten all of them...

FROM THE AUTHORS

This book was published much later than anticipated. Thank you for your patience with this series, and with us, but we had a baby!

Mari: Uh, what do you mean "we"? You had a baby.

Lila: I figure if I say "we" then it won't be weird when I leave the baby on your doorstep.

Mari: Yeah, I don't think so.

Lila: But she doesn't sleep! Why won't she sleep?

Mari: *hysterical laughter* Good luck!

Lila: *sobs*

In summary, it turns out that being pregnant and then having a baby seriously detracts from one's writing time.

But the baby is cute.

To OUR baby

PROLOGUE

She pulled the scarf over her hair out of habit. Her mind was thousands of miles away from the sun-warm streets of Istanbul, her thoughts of home, of Boston.

She held up a small laminated badge, skirting the line and the admission fee for the Aya Sophia. Called the Hagia Sophia by westerners, the museum was one of her favorite places in the world. Though hundreds of thousands of people visited the church-turned-mosque-turned-museum every day, it was far more than it seemed. Aya Sophia's secrets were right there, waiting to be uncovered—hiding in plain sight.

The same could be said of Juliette, and of the man she'd come here to meet.

Sebastian Stewart was waiting for her on the second floor. The crowd in the gallery was an eclectic mix of people and styles of dress. From the back, with his dark hair, jeans and long-sleeved button-down dress shirt, Sebastian could have passed for a variety of ethnicities. Rather than tap him on the shoulder—though in this heavily trafficked place, in the less-than-strict Istanbul, she doubted anyone would have taken offense—Juliette stood beside him, close enough that he'd notice her.

They stood in silence for a moment, a silence that was anything but tense. Sebastian was one of her oldest friends. The kind of friend who knew all her secrets.

"It always awes me that this wasn't destroyed." Sebastian gestured to the Deesis mosaic of Christ, which had been preserved under Islamic decoration and calligraphy when the church was converted to a mosque and uncovered during restoration in the twentieth century.

"It's nice when history preserves rather than destroys," she added.

Their conversation paused as a Japanese tour group stopped just behind them, the guide gesturing to the gold-and-blue image of Jesus, quickly explaining his importance to the Christian faith before moving on to the subject of the restoration and the technicalities involved in uncovering this and other mosaics.

"Chai?" Seb asked.

"Actually, I'm hungry."

Juliette followed her friend out then took the lead. Moving away from the tourist areas surrounding the Hagia Sophia and the Blue Mosque, she headed for a little hole-in-the-wall restaurant, ordering two spiced-lamb flatbreads. A boy with thick black lashes brought them *lahmacun* and cans of Coke.

Juliette ripped hers in half then took a bite of the soft middle section. Her thoughts drifted back to Boston and her stomach clenched.

"Are we going to talk about it?" Sebastian asked.

She looked up to see his meal mostly gone, while she'd had only a few bites.

"My brother called."

Sebastian froze, can halfway to his lips. "Harrison called? Why?"

Juliette pulled her scarf off, the fabric she'd wound around her neck and over her head suddenly suffocating.

"It seems my oh-so-proper brother made a mistake."

"The Grand Master doesn't make mistakes." He said it the way one states a fact—the sun rises in the east, the sky is blue, the Grand Master of the Trinity Masters doesn't make mistakes.

"He hadn't joined a trinity."

Sebastian sat back. "I hadn't realized he was that old."

Juliette nodded. At forty-five, her brother Harrison was twenty years older than Juliette. Not surprising, since her mother had been nearly fifteen years younger than Juliette's father, the Grand Master before Harrison, while Harrison's mother had been the same age as their father.

"Well, it seemed that Harrison did make a mistake—and not just failing to join a trinity."

"Oh?"

"He fell in love with a woman who wasn't in the Trinity Masters."

Sebastian whistled.

"Better than that. She was offered membership but refused."

Sebastian blinked.

"And he was willing to quit to be with her."

Shock froze Sebastian in place, and Juliette took advantage of the moment to take a few bites. Talking about it—and seeing Sebastian's reaction—was making her feel better.

Sebastian understood in a way that very few people would. They'd grown up together, children who were taught not to be truthful and honest, but how to keep secrets and avoid questions about their parents and home lives.

Juliette and Sebastian were legacies of the Trinity Masters, America's oldest and most powerful secret society. The society had been established as the country was born. Members were given unparalleled access to the resources and support of other members. Joining was a guarantee of success, and members excelled in every type of industry, from politics to art and science. The founders had seen the potential to strengthen the foundation of the new republic by taking the best and brightest Americans and having them support each other.

But there was more to it than a vague idea of support. Members had to agree to an arranged marriage—the price of security and success was their choice in who they'd marry.

And marriages between members of the Trinity Masters weren't arranged between two people, but three.

Sebastian had finally found his voice. "Are we talking about the same Harrison?"

"Apparently he'd been in love with this woman forever and was willing to risk it all to be with her."

"Is he...I mean, have his councilors..." Sebastian had lowered his voice, and the skin around his eyes was tight with concern.

Breaking any of the laws of the Trinity Masters was very risky. Harsh punishments were meted out to any who disobeyed. One of those laws was that once the Grand Master had assigned someone to a trinity—usually in their late twenties or early thirties—they had thirty days to marry, even if they'd never met their partners before. Since the Grand Master was the one person who could choose his own trinity, there was an age limit by which he had to marry. Other rules included no divorce unless necessary for secrecy's sake or other political reasons, and no discussing the Trinity Masters with outsiders.

Disobedience was almost unheard of. Juliette had grown up trading whispered stories about what had happened to people who broke the rules—framed for hideous crimes and locked up for life, scandals created that ruined careers, bank accounts drained, and spouses and children forbidden from ever speaking to the offenders again. They were the Trinity Masters' version of the boogeyman tales.

To break a rule was nearly unheard of. For the Grand Master to do so was...inconceivable.

"The woman joined. He's married now. To one of his councilors, Michael, and Alexis—she's a doctor."

"She joined?"

"Yes."

"But?" Sebastian gestured for her to continue. He knew that couldn't be the end of the story.

"But his other councilors forced him to step down as Grand Master."

"Holy fuck." He went on in several languages, not true cursing but using amusing, if vulgar expressions of astonishment.

Juliette snorted out a laugh. "Bastian, such language."

Sebastian glared at her. He hated the nickname. "My apologies, Ms. Adams."

Juliette bared her teeth. She hated her last name because it reminded her of her father, of who she'd grown up as—the daughter of the Grand Master.

The brief moment of amusement disappeared. Everything she'd told Sebastian was background information. The really shocking bit she had yet to say out loud.

"Does everyone know?" Sebastian asked.

Juliette shook her head. "They're trying to keep it quiet."

"That's safer; if anyone thought there was a power—"

Sebastian's teeth snapped together as he stopped speaking abruptly. His gaze met Juliette's.

"Jules," he whispered, using an old childhood nickname, "who is the new Grand Master?"

Juliette Adams took a deep breath. "I am."

CHAPTER ONE

Boston was cold in the winter. The terminal doors opened, allowing a blast of freezing air to flood the otherwise warm building. Juliette stopped in her tracks, hunching her shoulders and wishing she was wearing more than a loose sweater and thin scarf.

She'd lived here until she was eighteen but in the seven years since, Juliette had spent most of her time in Europe, South America and the Middle East. Except for a semester at St. Andrew's in Scotland, she'd been in temperate climates. She no longer had the constitution for a New England winter.

Gritting her teeth, she dashed out, quickly spotting the cab she'd called for while still in line to clear customs.

"You need a coat." The driver, who looked to be about Juliette's age, turned to examine her shivering in the backseat.

"It's been a while since I was in Boston."

"I'll turn up the heat. Where are you headed?"

"Charlestown." For a horrible second Juliette couldn't remember the address, it had been so long since she'd used it, but then the information popped into her head and she rattled it off.

The trip was slow due to the slushy roads and Boston's world famous traffic. The driver updated her on the weather forecast—for Bostonians, talking about the weather was not a matter of idle chatter but life-or-death information, and for a moment she felt like she was home.

They pulled up outside a three-story red-brick building not far from Winthrop Square.

"Here?" The driver peered at her in the rearview mirror then glanced at the expensive address in one of Boston's oldest neighborhoods. The travel-rumpled woman with her hair in a messy braid and a battered duffle bag did not fit the picture of the type of person who lived in a home like this.

"Yes. Thanks." Juliette made the payment with her smartphone—which was now several models old and battered from being hauled all over the world—and slid out of the cab, tugging her bag with her.

A keypad at the entrance required a ten-digit code plus a fingerprint. It unlocked with a discreet click, and Juliette pulled the heavy front door open. The lights were on but the heat wasn't, which more than likely meant no one else was staying here, but she called out, "Hello?"

Her voice echoed in the two-story foyer, tastefully decorated with antique furnishings and expensive art. It looked like any other upscale home in the neighborhood, but she doubted any of those other homes had nicknames like this one. It had been called the "frat house," the "fortress of solitude" and the "legacy halfway house."

There was no response to her voice, so she used a second keypad just inside the door to turn on the house systems, which were monitored remotely by a property management company. She felt the first waves of warm air when she reached the second-floor landing and the door to her room. There were six bedrooms and several dens. She, Sebastian and five other legacy kids from some of the oldest Trinity Masters' families had gotten together to purchase the property as a home base in Boston. For her and Sebastian, who had careers that kept them overseas, it served as a permanent address and a place to store things, like designer clothes appropriate for Trinity Masters' events, and winter clothes they didn't need anywhere else.

Juliette could have kept a room in her father's house, but even in high school she'd wanted nothing more than to distance herself from her family and its secrets and responsibilities. As far as the public knew, she was the only child of a famous actress, her paternity unknown. After her father had died, she'd politely declined Harrison's offer to keep a room for her. She'd had no choice but to live in the Grand Master's home when she'd visited her father. There wasn't a snowball's chance in hell she'd continue to live in the Grand Master's house if she had other options.

Her room was both elegant and sparse—a bare mattress under a protective plastic sheet sat on a four-poster wood frame. Stacked storage boxes were neatly arranged against the far wall, and the clothes in the closet were hidden in hanging garment bags.

Juliette dropped her duffle and considered just curling up in her clothes on the mattress, but she'd traveled enough to know that she'd feel better tomorrow if she put in some effort now.

She pulled out clean sheets and made the bed then jumped into a quick shower. It wasn't until she'd dropped onto the bed wearing a pair of flannel pajamas pulled from a neatly labeled bin that she realized she'd forgotten a pillow. Too tired to care, she propped her head on one arm and for the first time since she'd landed, opened her email.

The message she expected was there.

Juliette,

Please let me know when you reach Boston. We need to discuss next steps. I'd like for you to meet Alexis.

Safe travels.

Harrison

She dropped the phone to the mattress and took several deep breaths, giving herself time to sort out what she was feeling. Shock had kept her numb from the time Harrison had called until she'd met with Sebastian in Istanbul. An afternoon spent talking to Seb had pushed her past shock over hearing about her too-proper brother's out-of-character actions, to growing horror and anger over the reality of what becoming Grand Master would do to her life. She'd boarded the plane with jaw clenched—long-buried anger and resentment resurfacing.

That anger, dulled by travel, came roaring back as soon as she saw her brother's name.

Harrison,

Let's postpone the reunion. I'm in Boston and can meet with you and any councilors tomorrow after noon.

J.

Tossing her phone to the corner of the bed, Juliette closed her eyes then curled her legs up to her chest, feeling small and alone in the big house.

JULIETTE KEPT her expression carefully blank as she looked around the Grand Master's office. The room was windowless, as were all the rooms in the Trinity Masters' headquarters, located deep under the Boston Public Library.

She had been in here several times with her father, which,

while not forbidden, had been unusual. Trinity Masters' events were not family affairs; more often than not the children ended up together at one residence or another with the nannies or au pairs watching them while their parents attended meetings or galas. Only rarely had circumstances aligned so she was under the sole care of her father, leaving him with no choice but to not only bring her with him to headquarters, but into the sacred Grand Master's office.

In her father's time the office had been a musty, secretive room. Under her brother's rule the room had a homier feel, like an avuncular professor's office, but was tidy and well organized. There was even a computer, which Juliette's father had never used. It made sense, since her brother was a professor, and she'd heard from Seb that limited digital communications were now allowed, due in part to the fact that some of the best digital security people in the world were members.

There was still an air of mystery—with no overhead lights, the various table lamps with their heavy leather shades left large pools of shadow. The room had a midnight feel, as if the dark and dangerous night waited outside the walls. She gave herself a quick mental smack. It was one o'clock, and the sunlight against the snow-covered ground had been blindingly white on the way in. She was an adult, not a child to be cowed by shadows.

"Juliette." Harrison rose not from the seat behind the desk, but from one of the chairs around a small meeting table. "Can I take your coat?"

Juliette turned on one heel, letting Harrison tug her cream cashmere trench off her shoulders. She wore a trim wool dress in eggplant with elbow-length sleeves, black tights and black boots. The dress was a bit snug—she needed to lay off the feta cheese, olives and bread, which she'd regularly consumed for all meals in Bulgaria and Turkey—but not obscenely so. Her only jewelry was a gold collar necklace with a stamped triquetra in the center. It was the symbol of the Trinity Masters, worn to signify her membership and identify her to other members.

She waited for her brother to hang the coat on the stand in the corner before greeting him. "Harrison."

They pressed their cheeks together and Harrison squeezed her hands. Juliette tugged them from his grip then turned to face the other men who'd risen when she entered. Price Bennett she recognized vaguely—he was the CEO of a major security firm. Michael she knew—he was Harrison's best friend and now husband.

Price got a handshake, Michael a hug, but she didn't let the greetings last too long. Juliette sat in the previously vacant chair. The men looked at each other before resuming their seats.

That look—men acknowledging that they now had to deal with a petite blonde "girl" and they'd rather not—was one she'd seen a thousand times before. Icy calm coated her, and she swallowed the hot words she'd been practicing all morning. An angry rant was the last thing this situation needed—if she was going to do this, she had to take command. Starting now.

"Juliette, thank you for coming back so quickly. I hope it didn't cause too much trouble." Harrison was smiling slightly, the sort of uncomfortable expression he'd always worn around her.

She remembered when she was little wanting nothing more than to spend time with her handsome older brother, but their age difference was too large for them to have been companions. Later she'd realized that there had been tension in their parents' trinity, a tension she hadn't understood, but which Harrison had been all too aware of. Their disparate knowledge, along with the twenty-year age gap, meant they had never been close.

"I wasn't going to solve Eastern Europe's human trafficking problem in the next four days."

"Is that what you were working on?" He smiled, like a parent encouraging a child to report on their day.

"As if you didn't know."

Harrison sat back, smile fading. Michael put a hand on his arm.

Juliette placed her hands gently on the table, each movement slow and meticulous. "Tell me what you did, and what happens next."

Price seemed slightly taken aback, but then rubbed his lips, as if hiding a smile. She stared at him coolly, and Price dropped his hand. "I almost forgot you're an Adams," he said.

There was a moment of silence, during which the tension ratcheted up, her brother and his councilors seeming to realize that she was not going to meekly follow their orders.

Harrison cleared his throat then started talking. More had happened in the last month than she knew. Harrison's failure to marry and his decision to be with Alexis no matter the cost was only part of the story, and Juliette was horrified to hear about the death threats he'd received. At the same time his councilors had been confronting him about his failure to marry and relationship with a non-Trinity Masters' woman, he'd been receiving threats from an unknown enemy, who had first struck at more vulnerable members of the Trinity Masters. Though he had eventually married, his disregard for the rules meant he couldn't keep his position. Juliette didn't say it, but she found it romantic that Harrison had risked so much to be with the woman he loved. Losing his position as Grand Master was light punishment.

When he was done, Juliette leaned back, sorting through

her questions to find the most important one. "What does everyone know?"

"About the threats? Only a handful of people are aware. About your brother stepping down?" Price was the one who responded. "Nothing."

"Usually when there's a new Grand Master it means the old one has died, and there's usually some sort of ceremony acknowledging the death." At the first event after her father had died, Harrison had stood silent and unmoving before the membership, a lit black candle in one hand. He'd extinguished it before addressing the crowd. "It seems wrong to light a candle when you're not dead."

"The Winter Gala is coming up. Perhaps you could make an announcement about the former Grand Master stepping down."

"An announcement?" Juliette raised her brows. An announcement was both too informal and too ordinary for something like this.

"What happens if we don't say anything?" Michael asked.

"You mean don't acknowledge it?" Price shook his head. "The Grand Master's identity is unknown, but Harrison's height and voice are recognizable."

"If it's clear that there's been a change in leadership, but no death, people will wonder what happened. They'll wonder if there was a problem."

"You want to make this seem voluntary?" Juliette asked.

"Yes," Harrison replied.

"And will anyone believe that?"

Michael let out a startled bark of laughter. "I forgot how much you're like your old man."

"I'll ignore that insult." But she smiled—Michael had that kind of laugh.

Harrison shrugged. "Our members aren't exactly known for being the kind of people who can't put the pieces together."

"If that's the case, is stepping down enough punishment?"

Harrison sat back and his jaw clenched. Michael rose to his defense, insisting Harrison had sacrificed more than enough, but it was Price who really answered the question.

"I can only counsel the Grand Master, and stepping down seemed a fitting punishment. However, if you don't think so, then as the next Grand Master, it would be up to you to make that decision."

Michael opened his mouth to protest, but Harrison stopped him. "Price is right. It may not be enough. You're both biased, Price less so, but it shouldn't be either of your decisions." Harrison looked worried, and the way he glanced at Michael made her think that it wasn't for himself that he worried, but for the other members of his trinity.

"If I don't step in as Grand Master, who would the position go to?" Juliette looked at Price. He certainly had the personality and power to handle the Trinity Masters.

Price shook his head. "We'd have to check the laws. It's always been an Adams."

"But never a woman," she pointed out.

"Frankly, I think selecting a man over the traditional bloodline would cause more problems than a female Grand Master would."

Juliette nodded in agreement with Price. Anyone who joined the Trinity Masters had to be accepting of nontraditional relationships since they'd be expected to be part of a *ménage* marriage. Throughout their history, female members had been some of the most powerful women in the nation, able to rely on the strength of the Trinity Masters to push political agendas and break glass ceilings. Misogyny was almost inherently against the ideals of the Trinity Masters.

"While I agree, this is a break in tradition, and I'm young. Considering the condescending way the three of *you* were acting when I got here, I can only assume if I were to be Grand Master, it would be an uphill battle."

"It would, but Price and I will serve as your councilors, help you transition." Michael's tone was cool—it seemed he hadn't forgiven her for mentioning Harrison's punishment.

"I'll choose my own councilors."

All three men exchanged glances. Clearly that wasn't what they wanted to hear.

"The Winter Gala is coming up, so you have some time to make a decision." Harrison reached out to her but paused, his hand slowly sinking to lie palm down on the table. "Juliette, I never expected this to pass to you. I never meant..."

She met her brother's gaze and something passed between them. Others, people like Price and Michael, might think they understood, but in Harrison's eyes she saw the weight of the responsibility that he'd born, the same weight that had made Juliette's father such a hard man.

Juliette had come to this meeting knowing that there was no real choice. Price was right. Her age and gender were problematic, but it was her lineage that mattered most. She was willing, if not prepared, to become the Grand Master. Grudgingly, angrily, with the intention of making some serious changes, but willingly, she would take on the mantle of her family responsibility.

There was one aspect she hadn't considered, until now.

Juliette placed her hand over Harrison's and lowered her voice. Hoping only he could hear what she said next.

"I'm glad your children won't have to grow up the way we did," she whispered.

Harrison squeezed her fingers. "Juliette, I'm so sorry."

She leaned back. "I'm ready."

"Do you want time to think about it?"

"No."

Her brother stood. "Price, Michael, if you'll leave us."

"Harrison, do you need..." Michael's brow was furrowed.

"No. This is between the Grand Master and me."

Juliette shivered to hear herself referred to as the Grand Master.

Both Price and Michael, who'd been councilors to the Grand Master and therefore part of the already secretive Trinity Masters' most exclusive and reticent inner circle, looked surprised that something was about to happen that even *they* couldn't know about.

In the ceremony room, Grand Master laid the book on the altar—his final task in this role. It was a thin tome, the paper thick but old, some of its few pages cracking in the corners. He wore the robe of his office, black velvet trimmed in gold, face shadowed by the deep hood. A gold chain draped his shoulders.

This ceremony was rarely used, the role of Grand Master usually passing with the previous Grand Master's death. His movements were hesitant, like a man performing a dance he couldn't remember the moves to.

She wore a white robe, the kind worn by women when called to the altar to meet their partners. Approaching the stone from the other side, she moved with grace, lacking the hesitance the Grand Master showed.

The book was opened, the short list of names revealed. The last name on the list, Harrison Adams, was stark black compared to the faded ink and stains of the others.

Taking a pen from his robe, Harrison wrote his initials next to his name, signifying the end of his time as Grand Master. Using the sharp tip of the fountain pen, he cut his finger, letting a drop of blood well then smearing it across his name. A sign that this had been done willingly. Above Harrison's name, their father's lacked the blood mark, his shaky, nearly illegible initials a sign that he'd relinquished the chain on his deathbed. Only one name was struck through, indicating that he'd been removed from the position. It was a gift to Harrison that his name would not bear that black mark.

The now former Grand Master took off the chain, laying it on the altar then shrugged out of his robe. Juliette shed hers, unashamedly naked beneath. Harrison helped her into his black robe, pulling the hood up to cover her hair, putting her face in shadow. She might have been short, and a bit more slender than other Grand Masters, but the robe did what it was meant to do—render her the anonymous, powerful Grand Master.

Harrison covered his nakedness with a plain gray robe before continuing. Draping the chain over her shoulders, Harrison spoke their words. *"Mitimur in Vetitum."*

Juliette Adams, Grand Master of the Trinity Masters, took up the pen and signed her name under the bloodstained signature of her brother then closed the book.

Harrison bowed his head. "Grand Master."

In the shadow of the hood, he couldn't see the fear that twisted her face, or the tears that slid down Juliette's cheeks as she said good-bye to her life as she'd known it.

CHAPTER TWO

"You actually did it."

"Yep."

"You're the Grand Master."

"This conversation is getting repetitive." Juliette shook out a sweater dress, wondering if it was too dated to wear again.

"I'm trying to process." Sebastian's voice cracked through her earbuds. The internet call had fairly good quality, but he'd gone back to a remote area outside of Diyarbakir, where he was working with the Kurdish ethnic minority communities. One of Sebastian's strengths, thanks to his degrees in international relations and civics, was in helping communities make the transition to self-sustaining governments, an undervalued step in the process of raising a community from poverty and/or disarray to self-sustaining governance.

"How's your brother handling this?" Sebastian asked.

Juliette opened her mouth, prepared to tell Sebastian about everything else that had happened leading up to her brother stepping down, but she stopped herself. She was used to telling Sebastian everything, but things were different—had to *start* being different. Grand Master was not a role she could shrug off, even if it meant she held back information from a friend.

"He's handling it. Honestly, I don't think he's that sad to give it up. Now he can focus on his trinity. Have kids. Write boring research papers."

Sebastian laughed. "He can have his boring life. What I want to know is what you, all powerful Grand Master, are going to do next?"

"First I'm going to finish unpacking."

"Your Boston clothes?"

"Yep." She tossed a pair of artificially faded nineties' jeans onto the floor. "Most of them are still useable."

"Is anyone else there?"

"Nope, just me. Hopefully no one else will be around. I need some alone time."

"You hate alone time."

"Oh shut up, you know-it-all. You should be nicer to me. I *am* the Grand Master, after all."

His reply to that was an elegant snort. Strangely, that made her feel better.

"What are you going to tell North Star?" Now Sebastian's voice was somber.

Juliette sat heavily on the side of the bed. North Star was the human trafficking nonprofit she worked for. Since money wasn't really a concern for her, she wasn't on the payroll but spearheaded several projects, including technical training for cities and organizations that wanted to set up hotlines to report human trafficking for exploited women and children to call. If Seb knew how to implement infrastructure, Juliette knew how to work with and empower people.

"I told them there was a family emergency. I can finish up the project in Edirne via conference calls, and then I just need to report out to some of the mapping agencies."

"Do you have a lot to report?"

"Enough. I traveled with the local lead along the border areas."

Sebastian made an odd noise, one she couldn't understand until he spoke. "You might be able to keep working, once things settle down."

"Don't be stupid, Bastian." She used the nickname on purpose, a signal that she wasn't up to thinking about the future, and how different hers was going to be.

"But of course, oh all-powerful Grand Master."

She snorted, smacked her hands on her knees and stood. "Right now I'm going to finish sorting my clothes, check in with the business manager and then start going through the records."

There was a long pause, and she thought the call dropped. "Seb? Seb?"

"I'm still here. What was that last thing?"

"I have to start going through all the Trinity Masters' records."

"The membership records?"

"Yep. Those and the archives."

"Do you need to do that? I mean you don't have to go through all of those at the same time."

She couldn't tell Seb that it was the archives she was really worried about, not without explaining that the key to solving the mystery of the threats on Harrison's life had been hidden in their father's records. She remembered the dusty boxes of diaries and old files that used to fill the Grand Master's office in her father's time.

"Files are priority number one."

"Sounds boring, but you're lucky I love you, because I'm still coming."

"You're coming? Why?"

"You need my help."

"Excuse you. No I don't."

"Yes you do. Especially with the records."

Juliette frowned at the wall. Sebastian usually wasn't so pushy, or dismissive of her abilities. Chalking it up to concern, she decided not to strain their relationship by telling him he couldn't help her.

"You want to be my date to the gala?"

"The...oh hell no."

Juliette laughed. Seb hated Trinity Masters' events.

"Well I can't go by myself." Juliette made her voice breathy and feminine. "It wouldn't be proper."

"And you're always so proper. Don't forget I have those photos from the last time we were in Malta."

"Blackmail. Shocking. I'll have you know—"

Chimes sounded. Juliette stopped, the sound unexpected enough that her heart started racing.

"Jules? You okay?"

"There's someone at the door."

"So much for your solitude."

"I have to get that. Email me. Be safe."

"Be safe," he repeated, a sign off they'd used for years.

Hanging up, she quickly slipped on some shoes to go with her thick cotton lounge pants and too-large wool sweater. Sebastian had no idea how appropriate "be safe" was, considering the threats Harrison had received not long ago.

Reminding herself that only a handful of people knew she was now the Grand Master, she headed down the stairs, letting her sweater fall over her hands to hide the fact that her fingers were shaking.

Devon Asher tucked his hands into the pockets of his slacks, took them out, buttoned his jacket, stuck his hands back in his pockets and reminded himself that for fuck's sake, you're a thirty-year-old man, stop acting like an idiot teenager.

Once he was sure he had the fidgeting out of his system, Devon rang the bell, listening to the faint sound of chimes. It took just long enough for the door to open that he was fighting the urge to mess with his tie. Luckily, he was composed and still when the portal swung inward.

Juliette Adams was stunning. She always had been, and probably always would be. Honey-gold hair lay over her shoulder in a messy braid, her slight frame nearly overwhelmed by the knit sweater that was listing to one side, not quite falling off her shoulder but exposing the delicate line of her collarbone. Her skin was a warm gold, darker than he was used to seeing, and it gave her a sort of monochromatic-goddess appeal.

From fidgeting to flights of fancy. He really needed to pull it together.

She leaned against the door, blocking his entrance. It was ridiculous since he was a foot taller and 100 pounds heavier than her, but the look on her face made it very clear that if she didn't want to let him in, she wouldn't, and damn the logistics of trying to keep someone his size out.

He knew the house had top-of-the-line security, which meant she'd checked a video display to see who was outside before answering. That robbed him of the chance to see her unstudied reaction. Devon lived for the moments when he could catch her off guard, before her face and heart closed down.

As he'd been studying her, she'd been studying him. It had been eighteen months, two weeks and three days, since they'd been face-to-face. He wondered what she saw when she looked at him—if she saw him at all.

He was fairly certain that for Juliette, he was simply a representation of everything she hated.

A gust of wind tugged at his suit jacket, reminding him that he didn't have an overcoat. She shivered as the cold air whipped into the house and Devon shifted, trying to block the breeze. Her lips pressed together, a brief moment of...something, but then she smiled. It didn't reach her eyes.

"Devon, to what do I owe the honor of a visit from my betrothed?"

Damn it, damn it, she could not deal with this, with *him*, right now.

Stepping back she pushed the door all the way open and motioned Devon in. He carefully wiped the snow from his shoes before accepting the invitation. Juliette closed the door and leaned against it, taking a moment to center herself. She could feel him looming over her. At six feet one, with wide shoulders, he was physically big and his steady gray eyes seemed to always be watching and assessing.

She'd known him all her life and had been engaged to him just as long. Devon was one of her trinity, a marriage that had been decided upon as soon as she was born. Even on days when she was feeling charitable towards her father, Juliette couldn't see her trinity—herself, Devon Asher of the New York Ashers, and Rose Hancock, direct descendant of one of America's founding families—as anything but a political maneuver cementing three legacy families together.

It would help if Devon wasn't handsome and well-mannered, but he was both. His brown hair was only slightly mussed by the wind, cut in a classic style with a side part. His navy suit, blue-and-white checked shirt and blue tweed tie were both classic and fashionably trendy—eminently appropriate for a young D.C. lobbyist. A Burberry scarf was draped around his neck and he pulled it off with quick, efficient movements, turning to hang it on the freestanding coatrack.

"Can I get you something to drink?" The words were out before she had time to consider what she was saying. A knee-jerk good-manner reflex.

"Tea or coffee would be nice. Thank you."

Juliette bristled. "I haven't been in the kitchen yet, so you may be out of luck."

"That's fine." Devon frowned. "Have you eaten since you got here?"

"Five seconds in the door and already patronizing. Lovely." Juliette headed for the kitchen, throwing open doors as she went.

The less-formal living room was usable, but the dining room was draped in tarps to protect the furnishings. Everything was in place in the kitchen and it took her only a few minutes to find where the kettle was stored.

Devon had followed her in. She watched out of the corner of her eye as he stripped off his jacket and draped it over the back of one of the counter-height chairs pulled up to the massive marble island.

"I didn't mean to be patronizing, Juliette."

Filling the kettle, she had to resist the urge to slam the faucet handle. The way he said her name set her teeth on edge. It was the same way he'd said her name when she was a gangly ten-year-old, following him around and dying of jealousy when he hung out with Rose, who, like Devon, was five years older than Juliette. They'd been peers and she'd been the annoying little kid trying so hard to get their attention, especially Devon's.

"In that case, thank you for the concern, but I have, miraculously, managed to feed myself since landing." She went digging through the canisters of loose-leaf tea until she found a nice Assam. "Speaking of which, how did you know I was here?"

"Rose heard from Jackson."

"Who heard from Bethany, who heard from Sebastian. For people who live and die by their secrets, we're ridiculously gossipy."

Devon laughed, a warm, smooth sound. "True."

She couldn't even be mad at Sebastian—he wouldn't have said anything about her becoming the Grand Master, but he would have mentioned to their friends that she was headed to Boston. Not saying anything would have been suspicious.

"And how is Rose?"

"She's well."

"Still in California?"

"Yes."

Juliette watched the clock on the microwave, timing the brew. It gave her an excuse not to look at Devon as the silence lengthened.

"If you're in the states for a while, we could head out there to see her."

"How sweet, bonding time with your wives." Juliette turned just enough so he could see her flutter her eyelashes. For a moment his composure cracked and he looked irritated. Good. *She* was irritated; he might as well be, too.

"Yes, clearly that's why I suggested it, because I want to play lord and master over my women."

Now Juliette laughed—the way he said it, wryly and with a clear understanding that he'd have better luck pulling down the moon than being lord and master over either Juliette or Rose, was heartening. It didn't change the fact that their betrothal was a giant purple elephant in the room.

She poured cups of tea then motioned toward the kitchen door. "Let's sit in the living room."

Devon waited until her back was turned to let his shoulders relax. Sometimes they could go days stuck in a pattern of stiff formality and sly jabs. Other times...other times there weren't even words to describe the magic.

He brushed aside the nagging guilt he felt from lying to her—Rose *had* texted him that she'd heard Juliette was on her way to Boston, but that text had come a day after he'd already learned of her travel plans. Juliette would not appreciate knowing how he knew. It was a conversation he needed to have with her, but later, after they'd been called to the altar and their trinity sealed.

Hopefully, that wait was almost over. If Juliette was in Boston it must mean her brother, the Grand Master, had summoned her, and there was only one reason Harrison would have summoned Juliette—he was preparing to call them to the altar.

Rose had assumed the same, and asked him to text her as soon as he knew what was going on. Both he and Rose were well aware that the sticking point in their trinity would be Juliette, and it was something they'd had plenty of conversations about. He and Rose had a less-tumultuous, friend-based relationship, though her move to the West Coast had caused some distance between them.

So far, nothing Juliette had said or done indicated they were days away from the life-changing altar ceremony. Either she'd gotten even better at hiding her thoughts and feelings or she was being willfully blind as to why her brother had called her home. Both were strong possibilities.

He lit the gas insert in the elegant plaster-and-marble fireplace. When Juliette curled up on one end of a low leather couch, he took a seat in the chair beside it. He wanted to sit with her, to pull her onto his lap and strip off that sweater and...

Devon took a sip of the tea, forcing himself to think about something else. "How's your work with North Star?"

"Good. Challenging. It's hard to reach the people we're trying to help, and asking them to use and trust technology is an uphill battle."

"Is the planning complete?" Last time he'd seen her, she'd been helping to map out services and reporting lines that would mirror the routes women and children were trafficked along. They were trying to create a reporting pipeline that would allow them to not only establish how and when people were being trafficked, but allow them to connect the dots, possibly tracing and locating individuals.

"We finished identifying optimal geographic locations last year. I've been working implementation since then."

"What does implementation entail?"

She settled back, cup in one hand, saucer in the other, and started talking. Devon would sooner die than admit he knew most of what she was telling him—he was just happy she was talking at all. As she continued explaining, he could hear the rhythm in the words, a sign that she'd explained what, how and why she did this work before—to funders, to community leaders, to foreign governments. The way she spoke both told a story and invited him to be a part of the solution. It was a quiet call to arms, a gentle but heart-wrenching tale. The firelight made her hair glow gold and her eyes were bright with conviction.

He was reminded anew as to exactly how good she was at what she did, and how dangerous she could have been had she chosen a different career.

He asked questions, the motivation flipping from a desire to keep her talking to genuine interest. It was going well until she started talking about sneaking into a brothel and then onto a transport truck to get footage and firsthand experience that could be used by North Star for promotional and explanatory materials.

"Juliette!"

She jumped slightly. "What?"

"You could have been killed, or disappeared into some underground sex-slavery ring." Devon felt slightly ill. How had he not heard about this?

"That was kind of the point. I was wearing a GPS monitor, a hidden camera and carrying notarized copies of my passport. If they'd figured out who I was, they would have let me go. An American citizen is like a stick of lit dynamite—no one wants to be caught holding one."

"You just spent half an hour describing the kinds of horrors these women suffer and are surprised I'm upset that you deliberately put yourself in the way?"

"I'm not stupid or reckless." Her cup clattered against the saucer when she put them down. "I took all available precautions."

"Does your brother know about this?"

"Are you asking if my brother, who barely knows me, was aware that I took a calculated risk for a cause I believe in? Or are you asking if the Grand Master is aware that I did something that might compromise a planned trinity?" The words were cold and measured.

Devon told himself to calm down. He was famous for being able to keep a level head in the most horrifying of situations, and yet something about Juliette always got under his skin. He couldn't shake the mental picture of her being groped and hit as she was herded from a dingy brothel basement in Eastern Europe into the back of a filthy truck along with other terrified women and children.

"I'm asking if you have any idea how irresponsible it is to put yourself in harm's way."

"It's my life. My fight."

Devon pushed to his feet. "There are people who care about you." Bracing one hand on the arm of the couch he leaned over her. It was a bad move—the way her jaw clenched made it apparent that all he was doing was making her dig in her heels. "I know you don't want to hear it, but there are."

"I know that, but I can't, *won't*, live my life for someone or something else."

The fear of what could have happened to her was making him feel ill. That, paired with frustration that he hadn't known about this particular activity, pushed aside his normal reserve. "Thank God your brother brought you back."

"What are you talking about?"

"Maybe when we're married you won't be so reckless. Maybe then other people's feelings will matter to you." His teeth snapped together. That was more than he'd wanted to say.

Juliette slid out from under his arm and pushed to her feet, facing him down. "You came to Boston because you think this is it. We're getting called to the altar."

Devon cursed. If she hadn't figured it out on her own, this was not how he'd want her to figure it out. "Juliette, I..."

She turned her back to him.

Devon reached out, fingers hovering an inch from the bare side of her neck. "Juliette, if you let me, I'll make you happy." He stroked the bare skin behind her ear and down her neck to the edge of her sweater. "You know I can."

"Devon..."

"Yes?"

"Get out."

CHAPTER THREE

Paris, seven years earlier

It wasn't her first time in Paris, but it was the first time she'd been there without her mother. The freedom was dizzying, the whole world seemingly lying at her feet, waiting to be explored.

Juliette Adams—daughter of a celebrated actress, semi-regular player in page-six style gossip columns and blogs, member of an elite circle of offspring of the rich and famous—was here to take Europe by storm. The ink was barely dry on her high school diploma, but she had months of freedom ahead of her before she started college.

"Shopping or culture?" Rebecca Serafin was sitting cross-legged on the bed, maps and guidebooks scattered around her.

"Culture then shopping." Lisa Giese flicked her finger across her camera screen, examining the pictures she'd taken yesterday.

"How about we just wander?" Juliette turned away from the apartment window. Though she'd wanted to stay in a hotel—like a normal person—her brother had insisted that she stay in an apartment owned by a member of the Trinity Masters. Lisa's family wasn't part of the Trinity Masters, but Rebecca's was. As far as both girls knew, the apartment belonged to a Hollywood producer friend of Juliette's mother. Though Rebecca was a legacy, she didn't know Juliette's brother was the Grand Master, which was more than fine with Juliette. It wouldn't exactly be fun if one of your best friends found out that your brother was the person who had nearly God-like control over her life.

Grimacing at the thought, Juliette snatched up her jacket. "I'm going for a walk."

"Wait, we're coming."

"I'm leaving," she warned, taking dramatically slow steps towards the door.

"Coming, coming."

"*On y va!*"

Once outside, she let herself forget about the Trinity Masters. They wandered until they found a small neighborhood bakery, snagging croissants and strong coffee. Feeling like locals, they walked until they reached the river Seine, taking the steps down to the path beside the water. Trying to blend in, they spoke in French instead of English, turning their noses up at the tourists they passed.

"When are we meeting up with Sebastian and the guys?" Rebecca asked.

"Rome. They're backpacking right now." Juliette stopped to take a photo of a pretty bit of ironwork on a bridge, feeling quite artistic as she did so.

"Blegh. Why would anyone want to sleep on the ground and be dirty when they could be doing this?" Lisa spread her arms.

Juliette wouldn't have minded going backpacking, which her best friend in the whole world, Sebastian, and two other guys were doing before joining her, Rebecca and Lisa for the last two weeks of the trip. But then again, there was something to be said for a whole week of freedom in Paris.

They stopped to shop, Juliette purchasing a slinky silk dress that her mother would never have let her wear. She wore it when they went to dinner that night, deciding to eat at the famous Hotel Meurice. They didn't have reservations, but they were early by Paris standards and able to get a table without too much trouble. They ordered a bottle of Champagne—*real* Champagne, from Champagne—and delicately nibbled their rich, buttery food.

It was a glamorous evening—dressed in their recently acquired Paris fashions, dining in one of the most elegant restaurants in the world and drinking inexcusably expensive wine.

The only thing that was missing, the only thing that would have made eighteen-year-old Juliette's night the stuff of dreams, was romance. They received more than a few appreciative glances from men in the restaurant, but most were old enough to be their fathers. When they moved to the hotel bar, complimentary drinks arrived with semi regularity, and after consuming more than a few of them, the age of the men sending the beverages mattered less and less.

The drinks also helped Juliette forget that she was essentially already engaged. Rebecca didn't know that Juliette's trinity had already been selected. Normally members took advantage of the fact that they didn't have to go looking for their own long-term relationships by messing around. Rebecca was clearly going down that path—a well-dressed man had his hand on her knee.

When a slightly portly man in a pale gray suit put his hand on Juliette's back—which was left bare by the daringly cut dress —she smiled and played with her hair. Devon and Rose mostly just ignored her anytime they were together. Maybe if she practiced her flirting they would stop treating her like a kid. She was eighteen, after all.

"Parlez-vous Anglais?"

"Oui. Je suis Américaine."

"Maybe you will help me practice my English, no?"

"Of course, *Monsieur*." Juliette crossed her legs, biting back a grin when the man's attention dropped to her knees.

"You are, ah, in Paris for the vacation?"

"*Excusez-moi*."

Both Juliette and her admirer turned at the sound of a new voice—a voice Juliette knew.

Heart in her throat, Juliette froze when she caught sight of the man who'd interrupted them. Devon Asher.

His brown hair looked like rich chocolate in the muted lighting. He was wearing a tuxedo and was the most handsome, dashing man in the whole world.

"Devon," she squeaked, then took a sip of her drink to cover the unsexy voice.

"Juliette." Devon's smile was brief—there only for a moment before he shifted his attention to the paunchy man. After a second under Devon's stare, he melted away.

Leaning on the bar, close enough that his sleeve brushed Juliette's arm, Devon ordered a cognac in flawless French. When he turned to face her, Juliette could feel it. It wasn't just a matter of his gaze; it was the weight of his attention. She felt like a butterfly pinned to a board for study, except it wasn't terrifying, it was exhilarating. This feeling was totally new to her—maybe this was the first time Devon was really looking at her.

"You're in Paris." Juliette winced as soon as she spoke. What a stupid thing to say.

"As are you."

"I'm here with friends."

"I can see that."

Juliette wondered vaguely what the likelihood was that the floor would open up and swallow her. That would be preferable to sitting here feeling like a complete dumbass with nothing to say.

"Are they..." Devon spoke quietly, motioning to the others with a slight nod of his head.

"One of them. Rebecca."

"Hmm." Devon slid away from her, interrupting the conversations Lisa and Rebecca were having with their admirers. Juliette swiveled, watching as Devon ran off the men her friends were practicing their flirting on. Both Lisa and Rebecca looked at her with wide eyes, asking without words what was going on.

"This is, uh, Devon. He's friends with my..." Juliette almost said father, which would have been a disaster, since Lisa only knew the public story, which was that Juliette's mother had decided not to identify the father. "He's friends with my mother."

"Oh, are you an actor?" Lisa took a sip of her drink and tipped her head, hair sliding along her cheek.

Lisa was flirting with him. That bitch!

Juliette pressed her tongue against her teeth to keep from saying anything.

"No. And I'd hardly say I'm friends with Ms. Lissand. My parents are acquaintances of hers."

Lissand was Juliette's legal last name, Adams—her real last name—her middle name. She was impressed Devon had remembered. Then again, he wasn't the type of person who would make a simple mistake like that.

"But," Devon continued, "I've known Juliette all my life."

His attention shifted back to her. For the first time, Juliette truly understood the phrase "took my breath away."

"Juliette, would you like to go for a walk?"

"A walk?"

"Paris is best at night."

"They call it the City of Lights." Juliette wanted to smack herself. What was wrong with her? She normally wasn't this stupid. Behind Devon, Lisa and Rebecca were wide-eyed as they watched the exchange, but both girls winced at Juliette's stupid remark.

Devon's lips twitched. "Yes, they do." He held out his arm.

Rebecca and Lisa were gesturing and making faces, trying to communicate something, but Juliette couldn't focus on that. Instead, she laid her hand on Devon's sleeve and slid off the stool. He double-checked that Lisa and Rebecca would be okay, left money on the bar for their drinks and extra for a cab.

Then they were gone, away from the security of the hotel and her friends. She was walking through the moon and lamplit streets of Paris with her fiancé.

Despite that, she was expecting a lecture. Clearly Devon hadn't approved of the men in the bar. He probably didn't approve of her drinking, since she wasn't old enough to drink in the states.

"Did my brother send you?" she asked.

"No, why would you think he had?"

"I figure he sent you to check up on me."

"Knowing your brother, I'm sure he has people keeping an eye on you, but I'm not acting as the Grand Master's errand boy." Devon guided their path, taking them off the main roads into more picturesque neighborhoods where the houses crowded up against the street and wrought iron balconies looked like decorative lace in the moonlight.

"So you're in Paris for work?"

"Yes. Headed to Helsinki next."

"Do you like it, the consulting job?" After she asked the question, Juliette realized it revealed that she knew what was going on in his life.

But he didn't tease her. Instead he told her a bit about his job then talked about the master's program he was planning on pursuing. They walked until they came to the river, taking the steps down to the walkway. It was the second time she'd been here today, but now, in the moonlight with a handsome man, it was a very different experience.

Devon asked her about her college plans, but not in the condescending way other people did. She planned to tell him the same lie she told other people—that she was going to major in economics and international relations as a pre-law student, but instead she told him the truth. She planned to major in anthropology.

"You want to work for an overseas nonprofit?" he asked when she admitted her great secret.

"Yes, I mean, no. I don't want to work for a nonprofit. I want to help. Maybe that means I work for a specific organization, maybe it means I start my own, or do something else."

"That's smart, very smart." Devon's voice was low and almost sad.

"You think so?"

"You sound surprised."

"I figured you'd talk me out of it. I'm supposed to be a lawyer." When she got back from this trip she was going to have lunch with an old friend of her father's, Harold Martin, who wanted to talk to her about her career. As a member of the Trinity Masters, professional success was assured. Usually members were recruited because of their careers. Legacies usually had their careers handed to them. Undoubtedly this meeting with her father's friend would be all about him telling her what kind of law she was going to practice.

"Supposed to be?"

"Yes. You're supposed to be a lobbyist—which you're working towards. Rose is supposed to be a computer developer."

"Medical tech-development engineer," he corrected.

Juliette shrugged, trying not to hate Rose. Jealousy was death to a trinity. It didn't matter if that jealousy was romantic or professional. "The point is, we all have a part to play. And if I don't play my part..."

"Juliette, you know you have a choice."

She tried to laugh flippantly but it came out sounding rather desperate. "I don't have a choice."

"You do. Just because you're a legacy doesn't mean you have to become a member. You'd keep our secrets, so you wouldn't be a threat."

"I'm an Adams. Of course I have to be a member."

"I know your relationship with your father was...rocky, but Harrison would understand."

"Harrison might as well *be* my father as far as Trinity stuff goes."

They walked in silence until they came to a stretch of river where the trees on the street above were lit, their images, outlined in pinpricks of light, reflected in the sluggish water.

Devon turned to face her, his hands cupping her elbows. "Juliette."

Her heart was beating so loudly she was sure he'd hear it. His face was in shadow, and his shoulders seemed impossibly wide. It was almost as if a stranger held her. Maybe he *was* a stranger. This was not the Devon she'd known all her life. He'd never looked at her, focused on her, this way before.

"Devon."

"I want to kiss you."

"I want that, too."

"You do?"

"Yes." She spoke too quickly, too enthusiastically, and she caught the flash of white teeth in the moonlight. Juliette dropped her head in embarrassment.

He nudged her chin up with one hand. "It's been hard," he whispered.

"What has?"

"Trying not to think about kissing you."

"Why didn't you want to think about kissing me?"

"You're young."

"I'm not that much younger than you."

"Not anymore—the difference between eighteen and twenty three isn't so bad. It wouldn't have been appropriate for me to kiss you when you were fifteen and I was twenty."

"I wouldn't have said no."

"I wouldn't have asked."

"But you asked now."

"Yes, I did." And with that he lowered his lips to hers. The kiss was soft and gentle, Devon's hands slowly moving from her elbows until he could stroke the base of her neck with one thumb and press the other against her back. Juliette laid trembling fingers on his chest and hoped the moment would never end. When he deepened the kiss, she jumped. It wasn't the first time she'd French-kissed someone—she and Sebastian had practiced on one another—but it was the first time it had felt so good.

Devon pressed his lips to each corner of her mouth then rested his forehead against hers. He was breathing deeply, and she knew, she just knew, that he was as affected by their kiss as she was.

There on the banks of the river Seine, Juliette had the romantic first kiss of her dreams, and fell hopelessly in love with the man she would someday marry.

CHAPTER FOUR

The ringing stopped as the person on the other end answered. "Hold on, I need coffee."

Devon smiled, the screen of his phone a whirl of color and fabric as Rose moved around. It was six thirty in the morning on the West Coast, which explained Rose's need for coffee. She propped the phone up somewhere in her kitchen and he watched her moving back and forth prepping her morning caffeine before coming over to lean on the counter, staring at him through the video call. The gorgeous upscale kitchen behind her made him long for his condo in DC instead of the pot of room-service coffee in the hotel room. As nice as this hotel was, it wasn't home.

"Okay, give it to me straight."

"Juliette is back in Boston."

"And?" Rose's eyebrows, dark against her pale skin, climbed up her forehead.

"When I mentioned being called to the altar she told me to get out."

For a moment Rose's face relaxed in an expression that was almost relief. "So that's not why she's back?"

"Or she hadn't figured it out yet."

"Juliette isn't stupid."

"No, but she's stubborn, and ignores things she doesn't want to be true."

Rose shrugged in agreement, sipping coffee. "I guess we'll have to keep our eye on the mail."

They chatted for another few minutes, though the conversation felt stilted. Devon was trying to figure out why he was getting the feeling that Rose was either sad or worried, when there was a knock on his hotel room door.

Rose heard it too, and went perfectly still. "Can't fault that for timing."

Devon knew what she was talking about, knew what she was expecting, and he felt the same. They'd joked about watching the mail, but correspondences from the Grand Master were delivered by messenger. A young man with a bike helmet under one arm was standing outside his door. Devon signed for the large, nondescript envelope.

"Bring it over here where I can see!" Rose's demand pulled Devon from his blank-faced study of what he held. He took a seat at the small desk by the window, heart thumping. It was a standard document-size mailer. Opening it, he shook out an invitation-size cream-colored envelope. The front was embossed with the triquetra—the symbol of the Trinity Masters.

"Fuck," Rose whispered.

"Rose?" When he glanced at the screen, Devon was shocked to see the pain etched into her face.

She waved her hand then turned so he could only see her profile. "Open it."

What the hell was going on with Rose? Glancing between the envelope and the phone, he decided to deal with one thing at a time. He'd been waiting for this—had imagined the moment when he'd be called to the altar. Most members of the Trinity Masters didn't meet their spouses until they were called to a special ceremony. What he, Rose and Juliette had—a trinity arranged and acknowledged, if not formally announced, long before they were of the appropriate age to marry—was unique. Opening the envelope, Devon pulled out the folded sheet of heavy cream paper.

Devon Asher,

As of today, your previously arranged trinity is dissolved. Within the next twelve months, you will be called to the altar to meet your spouses.

Grand Master

"Devon? Devon?!" Rose's voice pulled him back to the present.

Jumping from the chair, he grabbed his shoes, sat on the edge of the bed and shoved his feet into boots.

"Devon, what's going on, why did you run away?"

He grabbed his jacket from the closet, moving on instinct.

"What did it say?"

He didn't answer, but plucked his phone and wallet off the desk and headed for the door.

"Devon!" She screamed his name loud enough that he heard it even over the sound of the hotel room door thunking closed behind him as he ran for the elevator. Holding the phone up, he looked at Rose, but the words wouldn't come.

"Where are you going?" This time Rose's voice was soft and soothing, coaxing him to respond.

"I'm going to talk to the Grand Master."

She sucked in a breath just as the elevator doors opened. "Why?"

Devon stepped in and hit the button for the lobby. The call

dropped as the elevator did. Rather than answer the inevitable call back from Rose, he held out the sheet of paper as he walked, snapping a photo and texting it to the woman who had, until five minutes ago, been destined to be one of his spouses.

JULIETTE YAWNED AND STRETCHED. She had no idea what time it was. The windowless office, so far underground, had thrown off her internal clock. She'd been too angry and keyed up after Devon's visit to stay at the house, so she'd raced to the Grand Master's office—*her* office. Though members couldn't enter the Trinity Masters' headquarters unless the library was open, they had a secret door that most people, including most of the library staff, thought was blocked off and she fully intended to stay here, immersed in the piles of papers, until she stopped thinking about what she'd done, about the notes she'd sent.

She was the Grand Master, the one person who had the right to choose her own trinity.

Why did she feel so sick at having sent that message to Devon?

Forcing herself not to think about it, she turned back to the notes her brother had left her. Harrison had been banging his head against the wall trying to decipher their father's journals. She wasn't going to bother with that—her brother didn't know it yet but she fully intended to make him suffer by assigning him the task of continuing to go through the notes—so she went in a different direction.

Every person, and every trinity, had their own file, all neatly arranged. Luckily the majority of the records were hard copy only, particularly the notes on the trinities. Even with the best digital security their members could create, Harrison had ended up in danger. That meant that the only safe place for anything related to the members was here, in the Grand Master's office. Having established that, now all she had to do was make sense of everything.

She'd been tempted to start with the current members' records. She didn't know everyone, and there were probably plenty of people waiting to be called to the altar, or who would benefit from the Grand Master evaluating their position and throwing the weight of the Trinity Masters behind their cause or career.

Like being admitted to a prestigious university, or joining a Greek house, the strength of the Trinity Masters was found in each person's access to other members. With some of the most powerful and intelligent people in the country on the roster, new members were treated to meteoric rises within their chosen careers. Those who held positions with nonprofits or who were doing humanitarian work had access to businesses and foundations that could fund their causes. Artists met the right people, had benefactors, and got the media attention necessary to pursue their passions.

Juliette opened a cherry-wood filing cabinet, running her fingers over the neatly labeled folders. "Asher, Devon" was right near the front. Seeing Devon's name made her stomach roll, so she closed the drawer. Checking through the other drawers and shelves, she familiarized herself with the contents of the office, tried to feel some ownership over the hundred-year-old books, brass lamps and heavy wood furnishings. Wondering vaguely when was the last time the oriental carpets had been vacuumed, she pulled up one corner and let it fall back, watching dust puff out. Coughing, she waived her hand in front of her face, turning her head aside. A small Victrola sat against the wall, the top closed. When she'd come here with her father, he would occasionally let her wind it up. Then he'd open the top and the two small doors covering the speaker.

He'd set the needle on the record and she'd lean against the cabinet, liking the way the music seemed to rumble through her.

She touched the cabinet now—it was only shoulder height, so much smaller than the massive thing in her memory—and for a moment her chest felt tight with the desire to go back to being a child, free of the heavy burden now pressing down on her. She opened the top and the speaker doors. Not trusting herself to use it, she gently touched the mechanism and ran her hand over the lower set of doors. A finger-length brass plate was screwed across both doors, holding them closed, just as it had been when she was small.

Juliette frowned, for the first time wondering why. As a child, she hadn't known—and wouldn't have dared—to question, but she'd seen her share of antiques since then. The larger lower section of a Victrola was meant to store records. Why was this screwed closed?

"You have so many better things to do," she whispered. "And why are you whispering?"

Letter opener in hand, she dropped to the floor in front of the Victrola. It took forever, but she got one of the tiny brass screws loosened enough that she was able to unscrew it the rest of the way with her fingers. Even then the doors wouldn't budge. She ran the letter opener around the seams, clearing away accumulated gunk and wood wax. Another five minutes of tugging and prying and the doors gave with a pained groan.

"Eureka!" she cried. Juliette shook the fingers she'd banged when the cabinet gave way. "And we have..."

There were two wooden boxes, fit so snuggly in the space they must have been made for it. Each was about a foot tall and a foot and a half wide, stacked one atop the other.

Envisioning everything from pirate gold to Area 51s' artifacts—both of which were the types of things that might end up in the Trinity Masters' hands for safekeeping—Juliette hauled out the top box and opened it.

"Oh good...more paper."

The top box seemed to contain aging manila folders. She pulled out a few and flipped through them.

"Birth certificate, report cards, doctors' records...these are dossiers on people." Flipping through some of the newer files—dated twenty-plus years ago—she decided they must be records for prospective members, who, for whatever reason, hadn't been offered membership. There were names on the tabs, and she recognized the illegible scrawl as her father's. The files were in reverse chronological order, and by the time she got to the bottom, the paper felt brittle and the birth certificates were dated fifty years in the past.

Turning to the lower box, she wasn't surprised to find yet more papers, but these were older—the paper yellowy-tan. Some were bundled up in twine, others in old-style envelopes. The penmanship on these was slightly better, but the ink so faded it was barely legible.

Juliette was flicking through everything idly, not really paying attention, when she stopped, fingers curled around a black-and-white photo of three mustachioed men. The man on the left wore light-colored pants and jacket, a scarf tied around his neck. In the center was an older man in loose clothing with knee-high boots, a rifle strap cutting across his chest. Next to him was a younger man with a flat-brimmed hat, his rifle held proudly in front of him. Though the hat shadowed his face, the younger man's posture and build mirrored that of the older man. The photo was tacked to a larger sheet of paper with photo squares, and the caption under it read "William Ludlow, Calixto Garcia, Pedro Garcia Fernandez."

"Ludlow. Ludlow and Garcia." The names were setting off

bells in her head. After jumping through several security hoops, she got the computer on the desk to connect to the Internet.

"General William Ludlow, US Army Corps of Engineers, fought at the Siege of Santiago in the Spanish-American war." Juliette's fingers were trembling slightly from a surge of adrenaline. "And then we have Calixto Garcia, general in all three Cuban uprisings." She had a tingly feeling, the same feeling she sometimes got just before she got someone to open up to her about their experiences, or before she put the pieces together and was able to identify where women were being held. "That leaves Pedro."

Leaping up, Juliette checked the archived member files. "Ah ha!" For a second, Juliette looked around for someone to share her discovery with. There was no one.

Sobered by that, Juliette pulled out the file labeled "Garcia, Pedro Fernandez." In it were a few other black-and-white pictures, several where Pedro was holding a gun, probably during either the Cuban War of Independence or the Spanish-American war. There were a few copies of official documents, including immigration papers from 1900. Pedro had settled in Florida and gone to school, joining the Trinity Masters in 1901. The timing probably meant that he'd been identified as a potential member and someone had helped with his immigration prior to his official joining. The bastard son of the famed Cuban general was exactly the kind of person the Trinity Masters liked to scoop up.

There wasn't much in his file after that besides some newspaper clippings. He'd been a politician and activist in Tampa and Key West.

Juliette switched over to the files about the trinities. More than just biographical, these files were meant to help chronicle the reason each trinity had been formed—a politician, soldier and socialite brought together to help shape military policy; an activist, lawyer and educator who together empowered social change. Locating the records from the early 1900s, she checked for one including Pedro. When a quick scan didn't yield what she wanted, she went through it methodically.

There was no file for a trinity including Pedro.

Juliette went back to the Victrola boxes. She'd noticed, but not really thought about the fact, that some of the bundled papers in the older box had three names on the labels.

It took her less than a minute to find a large envelope with faded handwriting that said "Garcia – Smith – Cruz".

"Why are you in here, and not with the other trinity files?" Rather than stay hunched on the floor, Juliette gathered up everything and took it to the conference table, spreading everything out so she could make sense of it.

Pedro Garcia Fernandez, bastard son of the Cuban revolutionary general, had been only seventeen when he joined the Trinity Masters. He'd fought in World War One, and been called to the altar after the war, marrying Lucille Smith and Maria Cruz in 1920. Lucille, a legacy, had lost both her husbands in the war and her only child to measles. Maria was the daughter of another wealthy Cuban family, and like Pedro, a new addition to the Trinity Masters.

Lucille and Maria each had a child, though their birth certificates both listed Maria as the mother, since by law only Pedro and Maria had been legally married, Lucille living under the guise of wealthy widow, next door to Pedro and Maria.

One of the sons had died fighting in World War Two. The other, Luis Garcia Cruz, joined the Trinity Masters in 1942. And...that was it. That's where the "official" file seemed to stop.

Several smaller envelopes had been stuffed inside the larger one. In those she found a marriage certificate for Luis and a birth certificate for his son Henry. Another envelope contained a copy of Henry's driver's license dated 1974, his marriage certificate from 1985, and a 1987 birth certificate for Henry's son, Francisco.

The last envelope bore Juliette's father's handwriting in the lower front corner. She squinted at it for a moment, before deciphering the word "inactive".

In it was a second copy of the birth certificate for Francisco Garcia Santiago. Behind that was a copy of a driver's license. The boy in it had an artificially serious expression, spiked hair and a puma shell necklace—the perfect image of a nineties teenager.

Smiling, Juliette flipped to the next page. "Well, hello, Francisco."

The photo was a professional shot, and seemed to be a color copy from the page of a magazine. The title of the article was "Next Year in Cuba: 100 years of the Cuban-American Experience", and it went on to discuss a new exhibit at a museum located in Key West. The caption under the photo said, "President of the Garcia Cuban Heritage Foundation, Francisco Garcia Santiago, will speak at the exhibit grand opening."

The dorky teenager was gone. Francisco had a lean face, slightly too-long dark hair, and startlingly light-colored eyes. He was smiling in the photo, and it was a quiet smile, almost reserved. The black suit, white shirt and black tie seemed a bit severe, but his arms were casually folded.

Juliette tipped the paper towards the light, examining his right hand, which was visible. On his middle finger Francisco wore a ring she knew all too well.

"Son of a bitch."

Juliette dashed to the computer again, this time searching for Francisco, finding a high-resolution version of the image in the magazine article on the foundation's website. She magnified his hand. There it was—the gold triquetra ring worn by male members of the Trinity Masters.

With a sinking feeling, Juliette spent the next hour checking the member files for anything on Francisco or his father Henry. There was nothing. For some reason, Francisco's family wasn't in the records. Luis Garcia Cruz, Francisco's grandfather, had been a member, but unless the file for his trinity had somehow been destroyed, it seemed that he'd never been called to the altar. And now his grandson was flaunting a Trinity Masters' ring in public photos.

Juliette read through everything a second time, committing it to memory since she shouldn't take anything out of this room. Placing all the papers into a new file, she labeled it "Garcia Family – Inactive?"

After a moments debate she put the rest of the hidden files back in the Victrola then gathered up her things and left the office. When she hit ground level, she pulled out her phone to call her brother.

"Are you sure you don't want something to drink?" Alexis looked at her husband Michael and then back to Devon, who was pacing in their living room.

"I'm fine, thank you." Devon knew he shouldn't be here—most members didn't know the Grand Master's name since he always wore a black, hooded robe—let alone where he lived or what he did. It was only because of the Asher family ties to the Adamses that he knew, but that didn't make this appropriate.

Harrison hadn't been home when Devon came knocking an hour and—he checked his watch—seventeen minutes ago. Instead, Devon had found Harrison's spouses, Michael and Alexis. He hadn't heard that the Grand Master had gotten married, but Juliette's brother had always been a private person, so he wasn't surprised. While Devon recognized

Michael, he didn't know Alexis, which made the fact that he'd invaded her house all the more awkward.

The metallic clack of a key in a lock made all three turn their heads. Michael laid a hand on Alexis' shoulder then left the living room, undoubtedly to warn Harrison about their guest.

Devon should be worried about the Grand Master's reaction to his breach of manners, should be worried about potential repercussions. He wasn't. All he cared about was an explanation. He wanted to know why his trinity—something that for Devon was as good as set in stone—had been dissolved. He wanted to know what Juliette had said that would make the Grand Master do something so drastic.

"Inactive? No. I've never seen anything like that." Harrison's voice carried faintly from the hallway. "You're going where?" There was a pause. "Do you think that's... No. Of course not. I'll try to think of anyone who might know more about it." A longer pause and then Harrison said, "Please be careful, Juliette."

At the sound of her name, Devon's already tight muscles hardened into blocks. He had to force himself to relax his jaw and hands, to make sure his posture didn't give away what he was feeling.

Harrison stepped into the room. Alexis rose from the couch and kissed her husband on the cheek. She whispered in Harrison's ear before leaving the room, closing the door behind her.

Devon hadn't seen Harrison in years. The man had aged; his dark hair was no longer streaked with gray. Instead, the salt and pepper was equally distributed and there were deep lines creating defined grooves in his face.

He didn't smile when he saw Devon. Instead, he gave him a short nod that, paired with Harrison's stern expression, offered

Devon no hope that this conversation would end well. He took a seat then gestured for Devon to do the same.

"You shouldn't be here, Devon."

"I know, Grand Master."

Harrison slashed a hand through the air, frowning. "Don't... Tell me why you're here."

"I want to know why you did it."

Harrison went unnaturally still. "Why I did what?"

The words caught in his throat. Devon pulled the letter from his pocket and held it out. Harrison took it, glancing over it quickly, then handed it back.

"When did you get this?"

"Earlier today."

"I assume you've seen Juliette."

"This morning."

Harrison was silent, waiting for Devon to continue. When he didn't, the Grand Master gestured. "And?"

"What did she say to you?" Devon rubbed his forehead. "What did I do? What did she find out? Whatever it is, it can't have been bad enough that you had to dissolve our trinity."

"You know your situation, the fact that your trinity was decided on when you, Juliette and Rose were children, is unique."

"I do."

"And since you've known Juliette her whole life, you better than anyone should know that it's been hard on her, for many reasons."

"It wasn't easy on Rose or me, either."

Harrison raised a brow and Devon realized that had come out more pouty than explanatory. He cleared his throat. "Grand Master, I—"

He didn't get to finish his sentence because for the second

time, Harrison slashed a hand through the air, his shiny new wedding ring catching the light. "I have to stop you."

Harrison leaned forward, passing back the letter. Devon took it, a strange feeling of foreboding settling over him. The expression on Harrison's face was one he couldn't decipher.

"Devon, I did not send you that note." Harrison braced his elbows on his knees. "And you should not address me as 'Grand Master'."

"I don't understand."

"Given the circumstances, you have a right to know, but I must ask you to keep this information to yourself. Members of your family are among the handful of legacy bloodlines who know that the Grand Master is an Adams, who would know my name."

Devon looked at the paper, this time really looking at the bold, cursive handwriting.

"I didn't send you that note because I am no longer the Grand Master." Harrison's voice was calm and smooth, as if he were relating the weather forecast.

Devon sat back in his chair, distancing himself from the words. "If you're not the Grand Master, who is?"

A small, sad smile twisted Harrison's lips.

Devon dropped his head into his hands. "Juliette?"

"Juliette." Harrison briefly patted Devon's shoulder. "I think this is a conversation you need to have with her, Devon. For me to say anything more would be completely inappropriate. Go talk to her."

Harrison quietly walked out, leaving Devon to contemplate the way his world had been turned upside down.

CHAPTER FIVE

Franco Garcia adjusted the contrast of the image, peering intently at his computer screen. Was that word "for" or "from"? The elegant feminine handwriting was the type of cursive where only the first letter was actually legible. Given the age of the letter, and the condition it had been found in—Florida was hell on old documents—he couldn't be sure.

Leaning back, he adjusted his reading glasses then peered at the real letter, which was between two thin sheets of protective Plexiglas. He knew the best chance of deciphering it was in manipulating the scanned image, but the impulse to check the original with his own eyes was hard to ignore, even though ten years as an archivist, and a lifetime as a card-carrying geek, meant that he lived for the latest tech gadgets and application of tech to his decidedly anti-tech profession.

It was time for a break. Franco rose and scratched his stomach. The humidity-controlled room was tucked in the center of the first floor of the mansion-turned-museum that was the Garcia Cuban Heritage Foundation. The lack of windows meant he didn't really know what time it was, but his stomach was telling him it was food time. Given the way Franco managed his day-to-day life—meaning he didn't manage it in any remotely adult way—it could be noon or midnight.

Turning off the light box under the letter, Franco slipped out of his workroom into a dim hallway that was closed to the public. The foundation offices, which really meant an office for the foundation director Marcia, were beside his workroom. Her door was shut, meaning that whatever time it was, the museum was closed.

He doubted there was anything to eat in his living quarters on the second floor, so rather than heading for the back stairs he decided to walk to the little twenty-four-hour shop down the street and get food. Franco opened the door into what had once been a drawing room and was now a gallery filled with memorabilia about the early days of the cigar business in Florida.

Diffused Florida sunshine had him blinking, and Franco lifted the hem of his ratty t-shirt, using it to rub his eyes. Daytime. It was definitely daytime, and he'd been inside too long if that little bit of light coming through the glazed windows was hurting his eyes.

"Hello."

Franco froze in the doorway and dropped his shirt. "Uh..."

She was backlit by the sun, hair glowing gold, her silhouetted figure trim and elegant in a skirt and blouse.

"Hello?" She added a slight upswing to the end of the word as she stepped forward. Franco was too confused to reply. Marcia's door was closed, therefore the museum was closed. This room should be empty.

His brain seemed to be stuck on that fact until he got a better look at her.

Once she was away from the windows, he was able to make out her features. She was beautiful, with large blue eyes and a golden complexion—tan, but not the leathered look fair-skinned people got from too much time in the sun. Her whole look was understated and elegant—she reminded him of the women in old photos. Because cameras had been so rare, those photos were usually meticulously planned, with the subjects wearing their Sunday best and standing straight and tall. Though her outfit didn't seem fancy, he got that same sense of upright planned elegance from her.

There was a hint of New England in her voice, and her clothing looked like heavy fabric—the skirt wool, the blouse some sort of slightly shimmery thick material.

Her golden-brown brows drew together. "Do you work here?"

"Oh, right!" How long had he been standing there staring? Long enough for it to be awkward? Undoubtedly. "I do work here, I'm—"

He took a step, forgetting about the stanchions and velvet rope that blocked off the doorway on the guest's side. Both stanchions fell over, the rope twisting around his ankle. Franco nearly fell, but managed to keep his balance, hopping on one foot.

"Let me help you."

The woman crouched just as he bent down, and Franco knocked his head into hers. She yelped and leaned away. Franco reached to help her, stuttering an apology, and instead lost his balance. Arms flailing, he managed to smack her in the shoulder before finally surrendering to gravity.

The blonde fell back onto her bottom and Franco landed on his hands and knees, his face an inch from her breasts.

There was a pregnant pause during which he could only blink, wondering how the hell he'd managed this particular fuckup. Seriously, these things only happened to him.

Then she started to laugh. The blonde dropped back until

she was lying on the floor, propped up on her elbows, laughing so hard she was gasping for breath.

Juliette peered at the half-horrified, half-bemused expression on the man's face and a fresh wave of laughter shook her. Of all the scenarios for how this meeting would go, the current situation had never been even a remote possibility.

Pushing his too-long hair away from his face, the man crawled backwards away from her, turning to sit on his butt and unwind the velvet rope from around his ankle.

He looked like a hobo, or a frat boy after a week-long bender. Baggy jeans with holes in the knees and rips by the pockets hung limply on his hips. He wore a ratty t-shirt that may at one time have had university lettering on it and a neon-green zip-up hoodie with some obnoxious cartoon alligator on the front.

Cut his hair, put him in a suit, and this could be Francisco, but nothing about this man said "Foundation President". If this wasn't Francisco, it had to be someone related to him, the resemblance was so strong. Plus, who else but a member of the family would be in the museum on a day it was closed?

When he was finally free, the man rose to his feet and reached out a hand to Juliette. Rather dubiously, she accepted.

As soon as their fingers touched, a shiver of awareness rippled through her. From the way he paused, eyes widening, she wondered if he'd felt it, too. It was chemistry, pure and simple, and she'd only felt something like this one time before, in Paris.

His fingers tightened around hers and she was lifted to her feet with a surprising amount of strength. Juliette looked up into the startlingly light blue eyes of this odd man and said the only thing she could think of. "Hi."

He cleared his throat. "Hi."

"I'm Juliette...Juliette Adams."

"I'm a grade-A klutz." He tucked his hands into his pockets with a self-deprecating smile. "Francisco Garcia Santiago."

"You're Francisco?"

Now he was back to looking bemused. "That's me." He grimaced. "We were supposed to be meeting? I was working and... I'll go find an usher, or Marcia—she's the director and you'd be better off talking to her anyway—and if you give me a few minutes, I'll find someone."

Juliette hid her smile. He was nothing like she'd expected from the information in the file or what she'd found online on the flight down here. "No, we don't have a meeting."

"Oh, well, uh..." He ran a hand through his hair, struggling to figure out what else to say. "Want me to find someone to give you a tour?"

"That might be hard, since the museum is closed today." She said it gently.

"It is? Then it's Monday."

"Yes," she confirmed, "it's Monday." Juliette fought the urge to grab him and kiss him. He was just so hapless it was cute.

"Wait...if it's Monday, how did you get in here?" For the first time he regarded her with suspicion. In Juliette's opinion, that reaction was very late coming.

"The door was unlocked." That wasn't entirely true. The deadbolt on the front door hadn't been engaged, so it had been child's play to open it. She'd had wire cutters in her hand, ready to deal with the alarm if her quickly gathered intel on the museum's lack of security was wrong, but nothing had gone off.

"Oh, uh, sometimes I forget." He was still looking at her suspiciously. "So you're just here visiting the museum?"

"No, I actually came to meet *you*."

"You...did?" He sounded both alarmed and resigned.

"Yes. I have something I think might interest you."

Reaching up, Juliette first took the clips out of her hair, which was half down after he'd accidentally whacked her on the head. She didn't miss the way his eyes lingered on her as the locks fell around her shoulders.

Opening her purse, she slid the hair clips in and then extracted the cardboard sleeve she'd placed the pictures in.

Wordlessly, she handed it to him. Francisco frowned but shook the photos out into his hand. He peered at the first one for a moment, before his whole body went still. Flipping to the next one, he brought the photos closer to his face then fumbled in the pocket of his hoodie, extracting a pair of thick, black-rimmed glasses.

They magnified his eyes cartoonishly and Juliette had to bite back a giggle.

"Where did you get these?"

Juliette opened her mouth, ready to start her carefully prepared statement, the first phase in a plan to suss out what he knew about the Trinity Masters, but before she could say anything, he'd turned and walked away, disappearing through the door he'd appeared from.

Juliette waited, but he didn't come back. Half-amused, half-irritated, she too stepped through the door, taking time to put the stanchions and rope back in place before following after the lost member of the Trinity Masters.

Franco jerked on his gloves, moved the letter he'd been examining off the light box, carefully laid out the photos the blonde had brought then flipped the light on.

Planting his hands on the worktable, he peered at the first photo. Three men. The one on the left in white, or possibly tan pants and a jacket. The older man in the center in loose clothing and tall boots, a rifle across his chest. Francisco knew both of them. Well, he didn't *know* them, since they'd been dead a long time. He recognized them.

William Ludlow was on the left, and in the center was Calixto Garcia, general in the Cuban revolution. Next to Garcia was the third person—a younger man wearing a hat, sporting a wispy mustache that meant he was probably only in his teens.

"Unbelievable," he muttered to himself. He needed to check the background against a picture they had in the collection of Ludlow and Garcia together. It looked as if both photos were taken the same day—the men were in the same outfits, with the same scenery in the background. In the photo they had on display, there were a variety of men standing behind and slightly downhill from Ludlow and Garcia. The third man in this picture had to be someone important to merit a photo with two such powerful men. A hat shadowed half the younger man's face, but there was something familiar about him, as if Franco should recognize him. He almost looked like—

"Pedro Garcia Fernandez."

Franco's head jerked up so fast his glasses slid down his nose. He shoved them back into place. The blonde—she'd said her name, but of course he couldn't remember it—gestured to the photo. "You were muttering to yourself. The third man is Pedro Garcia Fernandez."

"How do you know that?"

She took a larger envelope from her purse and extracted a single piece of paper. "The photo was mounted to this."

He accepted it when she held it out, vaguely aware that she was looking curiously around his workroom/office/library. There were four photo corners stuck to the paper, where the photo had once been, and under that, faded handwriting said, "William Ludlow, Calixto Garcia, Pedro Garcia Fernandez".

Ignoring the other photos for now, Franco took off his glasses and looked at the woman. She'd removed a pile of folders from a chair he'd forgotten was there and taken a seat, seeming tidy and elegant amid the controlled chaos of his workspace.

"What did you say your name was?"

"Juliette Adams."

"How did you get this photo?"

"It was in my family's papers."

Her voice was smooth, but something about the way she said "family" had his Spidey senses tingling.

"Why did you bring them to me?"

Juliette Adams raised a brow. "Isn't the young man in the photo, Pedro, your great-grandfather?"

"How do you know that?"

"Is it a secret?"

"Not a secret, but not something we talk about." Franco looked at her, letting the silence stretch out. He never minded silence, since his mind had a tendency to wander anyway, but he'd been told it made other people uncomfortable and had used that to his advantage several times.

Juliette kept a small smile in place. Apparently silence didn't bother her.

Franco broke first. "Come with me, there's something I want to show you."

Juliette followed Francisco out of the mad-scientist laboratory. He opened a door, muttered, closed it. He nearly tripped over his feet as he sped towards the next door. Throwing it open, he stuck his head through then motioned for her to follow.

The elegant front room was on the north side of the house, the afternoon light diffused. Francisco darted across the room, flipping on the display lights. Small spotlights shone on large glass panels that divided the room into sections. Each glass panel was printed with semi-opaque images depicting photos, letters and maps. Francisco tucked his glasses in his hoodie pocket as he stopped in front of one of the panels. Juliette waited until she was sure he was done moving before joining him.

"My family has been fortunate. My great-grandfather, Pedro, immigrated to the US, and through friendships with several powerful families, including the Smiths, he was able to build his business and assist other Cuban immigrants."

Francisco pointed to a photo of a young Hispanic man. It was a posed photo, the man's expression serious and unsmiling.

"This is Luis Garcia Cruz. My grandfather." Francisco's voice fell into a rhythmic tone of someone telling a familiar story. "He was born in 1922 and was studying to be a priest until World War Two, when he left the seminary after the death of his close friend Henry Smith." Francisco motioned to a photo of Luis with a young man in an army uniform. Both were smiling.

Juliette took a few steps to the side, pointed at another display with the header "The Spanish-American War". "But your great-grandfather fought in the Cuban Revolution."

"You refer to it as the Cuban Revolution?" Francisco seemed surprised.

"The United States was late to a war the Cuban people had been fighting for a long time."

"True." Francisco gestured to the image of Luis. "Grandfather told stories about how his father had fought in the revolution. But my grandfather was full of stories, some of them believable, many of them not. The craziest ones are mostly about Pedro, which is why we don't include him in the museum."

"They must be very crazy then."

"Well, one story is that Pedro was the illegitimate son of Calixto Garcia."

"Why is that an unbelievable story? Wasn't General Garcia

a rather famous womanizer?"

Francisco shrugged one shoulder. "True. That is not the most unbelievable story."

"Oh?" Juliette kept her tone casual and inquisitive, but her heart was pounding.

Francisco opened his mouth, but then shook his head, studying the museum display instead. The silence lengthened to the point of uncomfortable, and Juliette had to fight the urge to grab Francisco and shake him until information fell out.

The thunderous knock on the museum's front door was so unexpected that Juliette let out a yelp.

Francisco was just as startled, jerking sideways into the display, which luckily didn't break.

"What was that?" he asked.

"There's someone at the door."

"I should get that." He stumbled away, nearly tripping over his own feet.

Juliette took a few deep breaths, centering herself and prepping a new approach. These "crazy stories" told by Francisco's grandfather Luis may be tales of the Trinity Masters. To anyone outside the organization they probably *would* sound unbelievable. She needed to know more about Luis, since he'd been a member, but never called to the altar. There were too many unanswered questions for her liking.

Juliette was staring into middle space, sorting out her thoughts and questions, when the sound of a familiar voice jerked her attention back to the present. It almost sounded like...

Sucking in a breath, Juliette walked quickly towards the door Francisco had used, the voices getting louder as she approached the entrance to the museum. She rounded a corner and stopped in her tracks.

"Dammit, Devon."

CHAPTER SIX

Francisco resisted the urge to slam the door in this guy's face and boot the gorgeous blonde out on her ass. He was starting to feel like Alice falling down the rabbit hole—nothing quite made sense.

"Do you work here?" the tall brown-haired man asked. Like Juliette, the guy looked put together and preppy, his attire—pressed khakis and a logoed dark-blue polo shirt—practically screaming New England.

Franco wanted to hole up in his office—alone—with the photos for a few days. To spend a proper amount of time studying them. Since the blonde had brought him the pictures, it would be rude for him to rush her out of here, but this guy was just an annoyance keeping him from working on this new puzzle.

"The museum isn't open." Francisco inched the door closed. "Come back tomorrow."

The man's eyes narrowed and he very deliberately put one foot over the threshold, toe of his shoe against the bottom of the door. "I'm looking for someone."

"They're not here, because we're closed." Francisco vaguely wondered where his cell phone was in case he needed to call the cops. Since he lived upstairs, and the museum was more informative than value-heavy artifact-based, the security was minimal. There may be a panic button on the system keypad, but he couldn't bank on it.

"Who are you?" the man demanded.

Francisco blinked at the question. "Shouldn't I be asking who *you* are?"

"Dammit, Devon." Juliette's words were quiet but spoken with fervor from somewhere behind him.

The man shoved the door open, knocking Francisco back, and stepped inside. His gaze was focused on Juliette.

The urge to protect rose hot and sharp, filling the space behind Franco's breastbone with heat and sending adrenaline racing through his limbs. He put a hand on the man's chest, stopping his advance.

"Who are you and what are you doing here?" Franco's voice changed with his anger, and for a moment he heard traces of his own father's tone in the words. It was far from a bad thing —no one fucked with Henry Garcia Hernandez.

The newcomer's gaze shifted away from Juliette, and the muscles in his shoulders and upper arms tensed and bunched.

Franco hadn't been in a fight since he was a kid and didn't actually know what to do next.

"Devon, you shouldn't be here." Juliette appeared at Franco's side, placing her hand on his shoulder.

The man—Devon—dropped his gaze to Juliette's hand. His shoulders slumped.

"The two of you, uh, know each other?" Franco looked from Devon to Juliette.

Juliette was smiling but her eyes were hard. She wasn't happy this Devon guy had shown up. Franco placed his hand on top of hers. As their fingers touched, another shock of awareness went through him.

"Yes, we do. Francisco, this is Devon Asher. Devon, this is Francisco Garcia Santiago. This is his family's museum. Since you're here, you might as well come in. Francisco was about to tell me a story."

"I was?" Francisco decided that this wasn't an Alice-in-Wonderland situation, but rather like being in a Marquez novel.

Devon closed the door, his gaze still lowered, the tension between him and Juliette palpable. On a hunch, Francisco looked at Devon and Juliette's hands, checking for wedding bands. Devon wore a heavy gold ring on his right hand, but Juliette was ringless. So they weren't married, but there was definitely something between these two—a kind of tension that usually existed between couples in a complicated or bad relationship.

"Francisco, you were going to tell me about your grandfather's crazy stories." Juliette slipped her arm through his, turning him towards the gallery they'd been in.

"That's what you want to hear?"

"Absolutely."

"Juliette." Devon's voice was tight. He'd followed them in, but stopped in front of a display in the foyer that detailed the Garcia family legacy.

The poster featured one of the annoying posed headshots the PR person had insisted they get and which Franco hated. This was the one of him in a suit with his arms folded, trying to look like a pillar of the community.

"I know, Devon." Juliette didn't turn around or break stride, tugging Franco's arm to keep him moving.

"I'm sorry, but what is going on? Why are you both here?" Franco's tolerance for weirdness had just been met. This whole day was too strange—first Juliette, then the photos, and now this guy Devon.

"Francisco, tell me about your grandfather."

Franco freed his arm and turned to confront Juliette. "Why don't you tell me why you have those photos of my great-grandfather?"

Devon stood just behind and to the side of Juliette, like a bodyguard. She didn't respond.

Franco was a lot of things, but a man of infinite patience and tact was not one of them. "The two of you need to leave."

"Francisco, I just want to talk to you." Juliette continued to smile softly.

"You can come back tomorrow when the museum is open and speak with the director."

"But I want to talk to *you*."

"Why don't you tell me why you're really here? Clearly you're looking for something." It was a hunch, but the way Juliette's lips tightened said he was right.

Finally she motioned to a picture of Luis—Francisco's grandfather—standing arm in arm with his best friend Henry. "Tell me more about them."

"The Smiths?"

"Yes."

Franco knew he should ignore the question and make them leave, but there was a mystery here, a mystery he wanted to solve. Who was Juliette and where had she gotten those pictures? Why did she have them? How was her family connected to his? Why had this Devon guy shown up?

Maybe he'd get some answers if he gave some. "Henry Smith and his mother Lucille were close family friends. Lucille was particularly close with Maria, Luis's mother—my great-grandmother. Their patronage had helped the Garcia empire get off the ground. Luis had been studying to be a priest, but when Henry died in World War Two, he dropped out of the seminary and joined the army."

"Isn't your father's name Henry?" Juliette asked.

"Yes, he was named after Henry Smith, a tribute to my grandfather's best friend."

"Is that one of the crazy stories?"

Franco shook his head. "Hardly. How about this—I'll tell you one of my grandfather's craziest stories, if you tell me how you got those pictures."

"It's a deal."

Juliette smiled, completely ignoring Devon as he leaned forward and asked, "What pictures?"

"When I was a teenager, Grandfather took me aside and said that there was a great family secret—that the Garcia's had been selected to be members of a secret society that guarded America." Franco smiled as he remembered his grandfather's voice, the way he spoke with such sincerity. "He said that he'd even visited the headquarters of the society, been inducted in a secret ceremony, and then entrusted with a box and told to hide it here in Florida where no one would think to look."

"A secret society?" Juliette laughed lightly. "That *is* a bit crazy, but hardly the most absurd thing."

Franco wasn't listening to her. He was looking at Devon. There'd been a moment when the man's face had registered shock before his expression went blank and he placed his right hand on Juliette's shoulder.

The position gave Franco the perfect view of the ring he wore.

A ring that was the perfect match to one Franco's grandfather had worn until the day he died. A ring Luis had sworn was a symbol of his membership in the secret society.

Franco's heart started to pound. Maybe it wasn't the same

ring. The weird situation he now found himself in was making him think impossible things, and see things that weren't there.

He shifted his attention to Juliette—and her necklace caught his eye.

The same symbol that adorned Devon's ring, and his grandfather's ring, was dead center on Juliette's necklace.

"Francisco, are you okay?"

"My...my grandfather told me that someday the secret society would contact our family again, that they'd need their secret back."

"Their secret—you mean this box you mentioned?" Devon asked. At the same time Juliette said, "How would they contact you?"

Franco took a step forward, trying—but probably failing—to subtly get a better look at the ring. Devon dropped his hand. Definite fail on subtlety.

"Grandfather said that members of the secret society always wore a symbol. A triquetra."

Juliette inhaled slowly then let out the air. "The name, Francisco. What is the name?"

"Is it true?" Grandfather's stories about the secret society couldn't *possibly* be true. Could they?

"The name," she repeated.

"Trinity Masters. He said they were called the Trinity Masters."

Juliette smiled, but it was a rather sad expression. "Francisco Garcia Santiago, I need you to come with us."

"What the hell are you doing here?"

"Who the hell is he?"

Devon and Juliette stared at one another, neither answering

the other's question. They were standing on the steps of the museum, sunlight streaming around them.

Devon caved first. "I went to see your brother."

"Why?"

"You know why. I went to ask the Grand Master why my trinity," *something I've longed for my whole life,* "was destroyed."

"Destroyed? Don't be melodramatic."

He had to turn away. He didn't want her to see the rage or hurt on his face. Her easy dismissal of what they had, what they were to each other, made it abundantly clear how little she cared. For the sake of his own pride, he wouldn't let her know that his heart was utterly breaking.

"Imagine my surprise," he said, throat tight as he struggled to pretend he wasn't an emotional wreck, "when I discovered your brother is *not* the Grand Master."

"No, he's not."

"Perhaps I should be honored that the first thing you did was to use that newfound power to get me out of your life."

"Yet here you are."

Devon flinched, as if the words were a physical blow.

"As you can see, I'm here on Trinity Masters' business. There are people, families, who've fallen through the cracks. I came to find out what Francisco knows about us."

"He knows too much."

That startled a laugh out of Juliette, though he hadn't meant it to be funny. "You make it sound as though we're going to kill him."

"*You* make it sound as if that isn't something you could have done, Grand Master."

Juliette's laughter faded. "You thinking I'd do that reinforces the fact that you know nothing about me."

"I wasn't saying you would, I'm just—"

"He's agreed to come to Boston. I'll talk to him."

Devon wanted to offer to help, wanted to tell her he'd support her, whatever she'd decided to do, but he didn't know how. She'd made her feelings towards him all too clear. That she hadn't told him she was going to be Grand Master hurt more than he could say.

"Do you want to fly back with me? I borrowed the Hancock's jet."

"No, I have a flight booked."

He hadn't expected her to say yes, so Devon just nodded. Squinting up at the warm Florida sun, he felt cold. It really was over. The Grand Master had dissolved the trinity. He and Juliette would never be married, never be two pieces of a three-part trinity.

And she would never know how desperately he loved her.

This wasn't a dream. He couldn't rule out brain-aneurism-induced delusion, but at this point Franco was sure it wasn't some hyper-realistic dream. He'd been contacted by his grandfather's secret society—contact that came in the form of a gorgeous well-bred blonde and a brooding preppy guy.

The car service dropped him off outside an elegant brick house. He'd never been to Boston before, but Franco was sure this was an expensive piece of real estate. That fit with everything else he knew about Juliette and the Trinity Masters.

It had been two days since she'd shown up in his museum and turned his whole life upside down. She'd invited him to Boston and he'd accepted, knowing he couldn't possibly live with himself if he didn't investigate the situation. He loved a good mystery. Most people didn't understand that archivists were detectives at heart. Detectives who spoke with people long dead through public records, papers and photos.

The secret society his grandfather described was a powerful, clandestine, unorthodox organization. If even half of the things his grandfather had said were true, this was going to be a very interesting visit. Franco had used the flight as an opportunity to make a list of questions he wanted to ask.

He rang the bell, stuck his hands in his overcoat pockets to keep them from freezing, and a few moments later Juliette herself answered. He was slightly disappointed there wasn't a tuxedo-clad butler on the other side of the door. The foyer he stepped into was certainly elegant enough that a butler wouldn't be out of place. Though Franco's family had plenty of money and he was no stranger to luxury, wealth in New England looked very different to wealth in Florida.

"Francisco, thank you for coming."

"I don't know if I should say 'you're welcome'."

Juliette smiled and Franco's heart thumped. "Why wouldn't you say 'you're welcome'?"

"Because this might be a plot to kill me because I know too much."

He expected her to laugh. She didn't. And that was more than a little terrifying.

"I'll take your coat. You can leave your suitcase there, or if you're tired, I'll take you to your room."

"I booked a hotel."

"I assure you, there's plenty of space here." She motioned vaguely to the house behind her. Now that he'd seen the place, Franco suspected there were more than enough rooms, but having his own place where he could retreat to sort through his thoughts seemed like a very good idea.

He handed her his coat. "Do you live here alone?"

"Right now, yes. But I own the house jointly with some other people." She hung his coat in a small closet then motioned for him to follow. "I'm going to have to keep reminding myself that I should tell you the whole truth."

"What do you mean?" They entered a parlor that was a

lovely mix of antique elegance and modern comfort. A tea set was waiting on a tray and a fire crackled in the marble fireplace.

"I mean that this house is the home base for me and a few friends who are all legacies of the Trinity Masters."

"Legacies?"

She poured him a cup of tea. "Our parents, and in many cases our grandparents, are and were members. We grew up knowing about the Trinity Masters and learned to keep secrets from an early age."

It took Franco a moment to respond because when she leaned forward to pour tea, her silky top gapped, giving him a marvelous view of her cleavage. When he spoke, his voice was lower, rough. "That sounds like a hard way to grow up."

Her head snapped up, gaze lingering on him, as if she knew where his thoughts had gone. She bit her lower lip and Franco stifled a groan of arousal.

"Growing up in the Trinity Masters *is* hard, you're right; we make good spies."

That jerked his attention him back to the issue at hand. "Are you serious?"

"Yes. I am."

"Then it really *is* some sort of secret cabal running the country?"

"Running it? No. America is too big for that. Don't get all conspiracy theory on me." Juliette winked, but the teasing look faded as she kept talking. "The Trinity Masters was created by many of the same men who founded the nation. The goal was to ensure that America grew and advanced. The way to do this was to ensure that talented, intelligent people—everyone from artists to scientists—were supported and nurtured, connected to other powerful, influential people."

"Like a fraternity?"

"Yes, but it wasn't limited to the children of the super wealthy, though they were certainly included."

"How egalitarian."

She shook her head. "Practical. America was up against European nations with long histories, powerful families and alliances. The founders didn't think that the nation would survive if they waited for these allegiances and connections to grow organically."

Franco took a moment to think. "It would make sense that they would recruit my great-grandfather."

"More than recruit him, I think the Trinity Masters helped bring him to America, acting as sponsors and cosigners."

"You have records?" He nearly jumped off the couch in excitement.

Juliette smiled. "You sound like a kid on Christmas morning."

"I'm an archivist." Franco shrugged, refusing to apologize for his enthusiasm.

"I have a whole file that I think you'll really enjoy, but I'm not going to give it to you now."

"Oh, that's cold. Taunting me."

"I suspect once I give it to you, you'll bury yourself in it and I won't be able to have a proper conversation with you again for several days."

"That's entirely possible. I didn't realize I was that easy to read."

Now it was her turn to shrug. "I've been surrounded by passionate, driven people my whole life. I know how they operate. There's a saying about dogs and bones."

The conversation lulled as they drank their tea, but it wasn't an uncomfortable silence. Franco's list of questions was forgotten as he relaxed into the leather sofa, the fire and tea both warm enough to erase the chill that had gripped him since stepping off the plane.

"Tell me more about your work, the foundation."

Franco told her about his fascination with the past, the way he'd learned, at a young age, to appreciate the mysteries that old records could hold. It was because of him that his mother had spearheaded the foundation, which became a home base for his family's charity efforts in addition to eventually becoming a museum.

When the pot was empty, Juliette took the tea away, only to return with a bottle of red wine and two glasses. She held them up, asking without words if he wanted a drink. In response he rose and took the bottle from her, accepting the corkscrew she handed him. Their fingers brushed, and she didn't move away once he'd opened it. They were standing between the couch and coffee table, too close to one another for casual contact.

She held the glasses as he poured, a delicious tension mounting each second they spent so close to one another.

"To new acquaintances." He tapped his glass to hers.

"Acquaintances and their secrets." She took a sip, meeting his gaze as she did.

Franco battled the urge to grab her and kiss her. The last thing this already-complicated situation needed was for him to muddy the water. With a Herculean exercise of will, he took a seat. Juliette joined him on the couch, tucking one leg under the other in a much more relaxed posture than she'd had before.

They drank the first glasses too quickly, and when the second glasses were poured, he was able to focus on the reason he was here. "I made a list of questions."

"Very logical."

"But I think I would rather have you tell me the story."

"What story?"

"Your story. You know all my stuff. I want to know what it was like growing up in a secret society."

Juliette stiffened, enough that he knew his request either frightened or irritated her.

"My story is not a good example. How about I tell the story of *your* family—at least as much of the story as I know?"

He was in no position to question her, but something about her reaction to him asking about her life raised that same protective urge he'd felt at the museum when Devon showed up. "That's fair."

She settled into the corner of the couch, propping one elbow along the back. "Your great-grandfather *was* the son of General Garcia."

"You know that for sure?"

"No, but the photos, along with the last name and the fact that he was targeted for membership, makes that the most logical assumption."

"I'll accept that."

"Pedro Garcia Fernandez immigrated to the US in 1900 when he was only sixteen. He spent a year living in a hotel owned by a member of the Trinity Masters."

"Not exactly the normal accommodations for a young man just arrived from Cuba."

"And in 1901, Pedro came here, to Boston, and was inducted into the Trinity Masters. That I know for sure."

Franco shook his head ruefully. "He was only seventeen and had already had a far more interesting life than I could dream of."

"I don't know about that. I'd say this past week your life has been fairly interesting."

"Can't argue with that. So what happened to Pedro after he joined?"

"He fought in World War One—there's a copy of his service record in the file I have."

"Teasing me again."

"You'll be disappointed, because there's a lull in the records until 1920, when he was called to the altar."

"Called to the altar?"

"That's when the Grand Master summons members to be married."

"Arranged marriages." It was both a statement and a question.

Juliette raised an eyebrow. "I assume you know about the Trinity Masters' marriages?"

"Yes, those were always the craziest of the stories my grandfather told. He always claimed that was why he married so late in life. He was waiting to get his two wives from the secret society."

"We need to come back to that, because I have some questions for you about your grandfather, but let me finish with your great-grandfather's story first. In 1920 he married Maria Cruz, the daughter of a prominent family who was herself recruited in 1919, and Lucille Smith, a Trinity Masters' legacy who lost both her husbands in the war."

Franco set his glass down very carefully. "I'm sorry, you said he married a woman named Maria, and then a woman named Lucille?"

"Not 'and then'. I thought you said you knew about the Trinity Masters' marriages?"

"I thought... I assumed Grandfather made it up..."

Juliette touched her necklace and the three-point Celtic knot symbol. "Members of the Trinity Masters have arranged *ménage* marriages."

CHAPTER SEVEN

"Ménage marriages." Franco stared at Juliette, trying to decide if she was joking.

"Yes."

"I...wait. Lucille Smith was a family friend."

"Not quite. Your grandfather's best friend, Henry Smith, was actually your great-uncle. He was your grandfather's half-brother."

Franco picked up his glass and drained it. "Grandfather always referred to him as his brother but I assumed that was a term of endearment, not literal."

"Members learn to hide the truth about their marriages."

Franco whistled. "I assumed that part was just a story."

"No, the arranged marriages are very real." Her tone was half-rueful, half-resigned.

"Have you...are you married?"

"No. Not yet."

"Have you picked your, uh, partners yet?"

"Picked?" Juliette raised both brows.

"Oh, right, arranged. Forgot about that. The uh, what did you say, Grand Master? That's who picks?"

"Yes."

"And you don't know who it will be until you're at the altar?"

"You get a month to get to know your trinity before the official ceremony."

"And what if you don't like them?"

"It's not a matter of 'like'. The Grand Master creates the trinities based on the skills and potential of each person—for example, a research doctor, college dean and hospital administrator are a strong trinity."

"I'm having trouble believing that the kind of people who are members—smart, driven, successful—all just meekly submit to these arranged marriages."

"It's what they signed up for. The arranged marriage is the price you pay for the advantages the Trinity Masters will give you."

"What about you and the other legacies? You didn't choose this."

"I did. Every member has to consciously join. There are some people whose parents were members who chose not to be a part of it themselves."

"But they know all the secrets."

"They know many of the secrets, and they also know the cost of spilling those secrets." Juliette spoke quietly and firmly.

"Should I be nervous?"

"Because you know our secrets? Honestly, yes. The reason I came to find you was because I needed to know how much you knew."

That was a seriously sobering and slightly frightening statement. "I guess I knew more than I thought. I just didn't believe any of it."

Juliette didn't respond.

"Am I...a threat?" he asked. Consciously he wasn't, and it wasn't as if he went around boasting about the crazy things his grandfather had said, but he didn't exactly keep it a secret either.

"No. The Grand Master's main concern is figuring out why your grandfather, who *did* choose to join us, and who attended several of the galas in the early nineteen forties, was not called to the altar."

"Maybe he rejected the people the Grand Master picked for him."

"If he'd refused his trinity, there would have been consequences."

"That's an ominous word."

"I won't lie to you, Francisco. People who disobey or reveal secrets have very difficult lives. There are stories of former members who end up in prison, framed for crimes they didn't commit. People who lost their livelihoods, homes, and families."

"Well that's...terrifying."

Juliette laughed. "It's meant to be."

"In that case, well done."

"I'm sorry, I really didn't mean to scare you. How about we finish the bottle?"

"That sounds like a very good idea."

They finished the first bottle then opened a second. They each had questions, each needed and wanted answers, yet no questions were asked, no answers given.

As the wine disappeared they moved closer together on the couch, until they were close enough to touch.

Franco brushed a piece of hair back from her face. Juliette gasped quietly when he stroked her. "You're going to have an arranged marriage," he whispered.

"If you join, you will, too." Juliette brushed her fingertips against the back of his hand.

"I want to tell you a secret." Franco leaned in, enough so his lips practically touched her cheek as he spoke.

"What?"

"I want to kiss you." Brave from the wine, Franco let his heart speak. He'd never felt such strong chemistry, or such an instant connection before.

"Why don't you?" she replied softly.

"Is that allowed?"

"Allowed?"

"Because of the arranged marriage thing?"

"Usually members use that as an excuse to experiment and be slutty."

"Experiments and sluttiness? This gets better and better."

Juliette let out a slightly drunk giggle. She was gorgeous—eyes bright with mirth and wine, cheeks flushed, lips soft and pink.

Franco couldn't hold himself back any longer. Sliding a hand into her hair, he kissed her. Her lips were as soft as they looked, her body warm and supple as she leaned into him.

Franco tugged her onto his lap with his free hand. She straddled him, sitting on his knees, her arms twining around his neck. Franco's cock was like a piece of iron in his pants, and he both did and didn't want her to slide forward.

She traced his eyebrow with two fingers, trailing them down his face. He kissed her palm then tugged her down until their lips met once more.

He hadn't planned to do more than kiss her, but the desire she instilled in him was like a living thing, growing and growling a demand for satisfaction. Each time she gasped or moaned, he had to fight the urge to move faster, to take more.

Juliette pulled back, licking her lips. Franco slid his hands

—which were under her shirt just inches from her bra strap—out from under her clothing. They stared at one another.

"Is it just me, or do we have some very serious chemistry?" she asked.

"I'm glad I'm not the only one who feels it."

"Oh no, I feel it, too. I haven't felt like this since... Well, it's been a while." Sadness clouded her face. Juliette climbed off his lap.

"What happens now?" he asked.

"You mean with the Trinity Masters?"

"No, *querida*, I mean with us."

"The Trinity Masters come first. Always." She stood. "I'll call you a cab."

Franco stared after her. In the end, this meeting had raised more questions than it had answered.

DRINKING NEVER SOLVED ANY PROBLEMS, but right now he didn't want to solve problems. He wanted to get very drunk, indulge in a truckload of self-pity, and then pass out.

Devon raised his shot glass in a toast to no one, since he was very much alone in his hotel room. Juliette had, of course, invited that guy Francisco to stay with her while in Boston. She'd never invited *him* to stay.

Then again, why would she? She hated him. She probably hated him as much as he loved her.

Deciding he was too old to just pound out some shots, Devon poured himself a glass. It was cheap whiskey, so he didn't feel bad dropping a few ice cubes in.

So many things had happened in the past week that he wasn't sure what to brood about first. Juliette was the Grand Master. His trinity was gone.

And Juliette now had access to all the Trinity Masters' records and files. If she hadn't hated him before, once she went through his file, she certainly would.

It was late—or early, depending on one's perspective. The unplanned trip to Florida and extra time in Boston had thrown a wrench in several work projects, and he'd been up most of the night trying to get caught up, and making arrangements so he could stay in Boston until after the Winter Gala and possibly longer. He planned to be here as long as necessary.

Necessary to do *what*, he hadn't quite figured out. The one thing he was sure of was that he wasn't going to just walk away. He couldn't.

His hotel room faced east, and as he worked his way through the bottle of whiskey, he remembered another hotel room, another dawn.

PARIS, *three years earlier*

He hated dawn in Paris.

Devon turned his head, taking pains to move as slowly and quietly as possible. The last thing he wanted was to wake her.

Juliette's hair glowed gold in the sunlight that was starting to filter through the gauzy drapes. He'd forgotten to close the heavy blackout curtains. That had been the last thing on his mind when they'd entered the hotel room. They'd thrown open the front doors and danced on the tiny balcony. Well, she'd danced and he'd watched her.

Juliette had been drunk on Champagne. Drunk on Champagne was the only way she'd smile at him.

He was losing her. Or maybe he'd already lost her.

The sun rose in truth, a ray of light now arrowing across the bed. Her bare breast was the palest cream, her arms and face tanned gold. She looked older than the last time he'd seen her six months ago. It was the kind of age that came from seeing and knowing too much. He hated her work, noble as it was. Juliette had always assumed she was worldly, but had, in fact, been incredibly sheltered all the way through her first year of college.

But the girl he'd first kissed here in Paris was gone. Little by little she'd learned how the world really worked. She'd seen horrible things, tried and failed to fix the world's problems. And she'd—rightly—come to see exactly how much damage those at the top of the proverbial food chain could do to those at the bottom.

The last time they'd met in Paris, Juliette had once again delivered an impassioned speech. First she decried the US government policies, ranting about the damage the CIA had done. Then she'd demanded that Devon use his connections as a lobbyist to address a laundry list of issues. He'd promised to do what he could, reminded her that he'd helped secure funding for one of the two NPOs she'd been working with at the time. He'd had to watch as disappointment filled her eyes. He'd turned the conversation to the Trinity Masters, hoping to distract her by asking if she'd be attending the upcoming Summer Gala. That had devolved into a debate about whether or not members should know more—such as who the Grand Master was, and the wisdom of the arranged marriages. The conversation had not gone well, and her disappointment had turned to barely controlled anger.

This time she hadn't bothered with the speech about the ills of the world, and every time he brought up the Trinity Masters she'd changed the subject. She'd plopped down in the chair beside him and drank like someone trying to forget. And she had forgotten, at least for a little while.

Maybe this dawn would be different. Maybe this time she

wouldn't leave. Maybe he would have the courage to tell her things she needed to hear, things he was too much of a coward to say.

Juliette, I'm not a lobbyist. Juliette, I love you.

But there would be plenty of time for all that once they were called to the altar. Plus it wasn't fair to Rose—the feelings he had for Juliette were on a completely different level than those he had for the third member of their trinity.

She turned her head, stretching one arm up as she woke. In that second just before the light hit her face he leaned down and kissed her.

Juliette's eyes fluttered then opened. For a moment, a sweet moment, she looked happy. She smiled at him, reached one hand out to touch his face.

Devon waited, praying, but before her fingers made contact her face went blank, her feelings locked down behind a mask that seemed to appear with the dawn light.

Without a word, Juliette rolled away. She grabbed her dress off the floor as she rose, holding it against her chest.

Devon clenched his teeth against the pain. He just needed to bide his time. Once they were married he would tell her everything. There would be no secrets between them.

But he was tired. His last operation had been a total clusterfuck, and he'd needed this time with Juliette to recharge and center himself. As she passed his side of the bed on the way to the bathroom, he reached out, caught her hand.

He held his breath, both terrified and hopeful that she would sense his feelings—need, love, fear, desire.

Juliette froze, her torso turned away from him, one hand caught in his. They stayed that way, frozen in the midst of a pivotal moment, as the sun continued its invasion of their room.

Finally Juliette tugged her fingers, disappearing into the bathroom. When she emerged she was dressed.

"I called for breakfast," he said.

"Thank you." She didn't look at him.

He went to the bathroom, and when he came out she was gone. When breakfast arrived, he ate methodically while checking his email. Then, just as methodically, he picked up her untouched plate and hurled it against the wall.

CHAPTER EIGHT

He couldn't decide if the location was a deliberate attempt to intimidate him. If so, it was mostly working.

Franco looked around the dimly lit bar—except it wasn't a bar, it was a gentleman's club. Not the kind with strippers, the kind with wood paneling, fireplaces, hunter-green plaid wallpaper and leather club chairs.

The bouncer had asked for ID then checked it against a list. He could only assume this was a membership place, and that the man he was here to meet had made sure his name was on the list.

Franco wasn't sure what he hoped to get out of this conversation with Devon. He'd asked Juliette for the other man's number because Devon was the only person besides her to whom he could ask his questions. The kiss had complicated things with her, and before this went too much further, Franco wanted some answers, so here he was.

Instead of looking like a grown-up frat boy, the way he had in Florida, the man who rose from a club chair in a small alcove was six feet of intimidation in a dark suit and tie. Franco tugged on the front of his sweater vest, hoping he didn't look like a geeky high schooler. He had a bad feeling this sweater vest actually was a piece of his old high school uniform, but he didn't exactly have a ton of winter-weather clothes, so he'd packed everything he thought would work.

"Francisco." Devon held out his hand.

"You can call me Franco." They shook.

"Franco. Thank you for meeting me here."

"I'm the one who should say thank you. To you. For meeting me."

Devon gestured to the other chair and Franco took a seat. The chairs were isolated from the rest of the room—a perfect place to have a conversation about a secret society.

"What can I get you to drink?"

"What's good here?"

Devon's lips twitched. "I've never had a bad drink."

"Right. Guess that was a stupid question. Uh, I'll have whatever you're having."

Devon pressed a small button on the wall. "Another Glenlivet, please."

"I can't decide if that's creepy or cool." He peered at the call button.

"Cool. Always go with cool." Devon's shoulders relaxed and he sat deeper in his chair.

"I have to tell you, so far this is all exactly what I expected."

Devon raised his brows. "I thought you didn't believe your grandfather's stories? How is it that you had expectations?"

"I didn't believe, but I'm saying that if there were a secret society, this is how you'd want to find out about it." Franco gestured around them. "Sitting in a dark corner of a members-only club, having a beautiful blonde show up at your door. Hollywood would approve."

Devon laughed, but Franco had seen the way his shoulders tensed when Juliette was mentioned.

"Juliette said you had some questions?"

"I do." Franco dug the list out of his pocket.

"You wrote them down?"

Franco waited for the tuxedo-clad waiter to set down his drink—which was a small glass with a finger of amber liquid in it—before continuing. "Yes, otherwise I'd forget."

"I'm surprised Juliette didn't answer your questions."

"We got off topic," Franco admitted. Devon's shoulders tensed once again. Okay, there was definitely something going on between him and Juliette.

"I'll do my best to answer, but until you're a member there are some things you can't know."

"That's question one. If I'm not a member, why are you telling me anything?"

Devon raised his glass in a salute and took a sip before answering. Franco did the same and manfully suppressed a cough. It was whiskey. He hated whiskey.

"There are actually quite a few people who know something about the Trinity Masters but who aren't members. Most of those people are legacies, like yourself, who chose not to join. Our secrets are safe with them because they were raised knowing the consequences. Others are those who were recruited and offered membership but declined."

"People decline?"

"Not often, but it happens. Joining is a high-risk, high-reward game."

"I'm trying to imagine how that conversation would go. 'You seem smart; do you want to join a secret society? We offer you wealth and power but you have to marry who we say and by the way, you'll marry two people not just one.'"

Devon chuckled. "When potential new members are evaluated, one fact that's assessed is whether or not they'd be open to the trinity marriage."

"Why a trinity marriage?"

Franco finished his whiskey as Devon told stories about other famous trinities, including Vice-Admiral Horatio Lord Nelson, who'd been in a relationship with Lady Emma Hamilton and Sir William Hamilton. The gossip papers of the nineteenth century had called it an affair between Lady Emma and Lord Nelson, but it had been so much more. The three-way union had helped end the Napoleonic wars, and both Emma and William had mourned Lord Nelson after his death.

"It's like a stool," Franco said.

"Excuse me?"

"A stool needs at least three legs. Two legs aren't enough."

"Exactly." Devon hit the button and asked for another round.

"Rum and coke, and water," Franco yelled towards the place he hoped the mic was.

"Water isn't a bad idea." Devon stood, removed his jacket and even loosened his tie. When he sat, he looked relaxed.

"Good." Franco, too, relaxed. "You're not going to kill me."

"Er, what?"

"You seemed as though you were just waiting for me to ask the wrong question then you'd kill me and leave my body propped up here. It would probably take days for them to report me as dead. But you took off your jacket so now I know you're not wearing a gun."

"If we wanted you dead, you'd be dead."

"Juliette said the same thing. I'm going to pretend you're both joking."

"I just finished telling you that there are plenty of people who know about us and aren't members. The consequences for divulging secrets are enough to keep people quiet."

"Good to know."

"But I won't lie. We would kill to keep the Trinity Masters safe."

"We? Are you an enforcer?"

"Enforcer? No. But there are members very capable of killing someone."

"SEAL Team Six—are they members?"

"I don't know. They might be."

"You don't know who all the other members are?"

"No."

"Oh, then how do you and Juliette know each other?"

"We...grew up together."

New drinks and a tall bottle of imported water were set down, along with crystal goblets for the water. When the server was gone, Franco shook his head. "Dev—can I call you Dev? Listen, we're friends now, right?"

"Uh, no."

"Sure we are."

Devon blinked then burst out laughing. "Okay, sure. We're friends. You can be my weird friend."

"I'll take it. But back to my point—you and Juliette, there's something going on there. I can tell."

Devon knocked back his entire glass, grimacing as he swallowed. Franco's eyebrows crept up his forehead.

"I've known Juliette since she was a baby. Our relationship is complicated."

"Have you slept together?"

"I'm not going to answer that."

"Fair enough. But speaking of sex—"

"Which we weren't."

"—If you join when you're, what, twenty? And you know that you don't have to try to date and fall in love..." Franco trailed off, losing the train of thought as he flashed back to his last disastrous date. Apparently mini-golf was only a cute date-night activity for people under the age of sixteen and characters in romantic comedies.

"Was there a question in there somewhere?"

"Right. What do members do before they're, uh, called to the altar? Do they remain celibate? Do they date but keep it casual? Hire prostitutes? Juliette mentioned sluttiness."

"Prostitutes? What the hell...no. There are no specific rules, but once you join, you know you're only asking for trouble if you start a serious relationship. Most people continue to date casually. Some take advantage of the situation and indulge themselves."

"You mean no-strings-attached sex?"

Devon grinned. "And freaky sex."

"Freaky sex. Yeah, I can see that." Franco had a brief and vivid fantasy of Juliette wearing nothing but an apron making empanadas. His subconscious was a chauvinist asshole.

"What other questions do you have?"

"Huh? I'm still thinking about the freaky sex." Franco eyed Devon. He and Juliette were like a matched pair of beautiful people. Barbie and Ken but not so cheap. If that was their connection—they'd indulged in freaky sex with each other pre-marriage—Franco doubted the freakiness involved baking.

"Then can I ask *you* a question?"

"Of course," Franco replied.

"Are you going to join?"

That caught Franco off guard. "What?"

"If the Grand Master offers you membership, will you join?"

"Yes." He should probably take a few days to consider it. He should probably wait and see if he had any more questions. But now that he knew this was real, there was no chance he was going to turn his back on it.

"Are you sure?" Devon seemed dubious.

"Absolutely. And you know why?"

"Why?"

"Because I fucking hate dating. If joining means I don't have to do that, then I'm in."

Devon laughed so hard he had to hold his stomach. After that, Franco gave up on his list of questions. It wasn't until they stumbled out of the club to a sky that was already starting to lighten that either man realized how long they'd spent talking.

They called for cabs, and once Franco climbed in and gave the hotel address, he realized that he felt comfortable with Devon. The kind of comfortable that was normally reserved for family.

Maybe that was because in a way, Devon was going to be part of his family, or maybe it was more appropriate to say Franco was becoming part of Devon's family.

Now all he had to do was impress this Grand Master.

Who was ringing the doorbell at six in the morning? Juliette looked up from the membership file she was reading. Her resolve to keep everything in the Grand Master's office —in *her* office—had failed after the fourth day spent in the windowless room.

Grumbling, she got to her feet and trudged to the door, passing a large grandfather clock in the hall. According to the clock—and now that she was paying attention, the sunlight pouring through the curtains on either side of the door—it wasn't six o'clock, it was nearly noon.

She checked the security screen, smiling when she saw Francisco.

"Francisco, hi. Come in."

"I hope it's okay that I just showed up."

"Of course." Juliette motioned to her leggings and battered sweatshirt. "Assuming you don't mind my casual attire."

"I wish I'd worn my PJs instead of getting all dressed up." He frowned at his slacks, button-down shirt and jacket. He had a bag over one shoulder.

"For most people, pants and a shirt aren't dressed up, but I saw what you were wearing back in Florida, so I respect your effort."

"Ha, ha." He hung up his coat, a strangely familiar gesture—as if he'd been here a million times before. "But you're right."

Juliette steered him towards the kitchen. The living room was off limits since all the files were spread out on the floor in there. "Sorry I didn't call you. How was your meeting with Devon?"

"Great. I like him, he's a cool guy."

"Did you get your questions answered?"

"Most of them, but then I thought of more."

"Oh. I've been kind of busy with work, so I might not be able to take time to answer them right now."

"Not a problem. I didn't come by because of the questions."

"You didn't?"

"No. I was worried. It's been nearly a week and I was starting to think something had happened to you. Like maybe you'd been silenced for telling me too much."

"A week? That can't be...what day is it?"

"It's Wednesday."

"Wednesday?" Juliette patted her pockets. Where was her phone? "It can't be Wednesday."

Franco pulled out *his* phone, flipped to the calendar and then held it out. It was Wednesday. She'd buried herself in the files and records for days—more days than she'd realized.

"Crap." She laid her arms on the counter then dropped her head onto them. "The gala is in three days."

"What was that?"

She straightened and brushed her hair back from her face. "The gala—it's on Saturday."

"Right. The Winter Gala. One of four annual gatherings."

"You sound like you're reciting."

"Just checking to make sure that I remembered everything Dev told me. I wanted to take notes, but figured that wouldn't be a good idea."

"Smart." Now that she wasn't focused on work, exhaustion was dragging at her arms and legs. Refusing to give in, she started making tea, selecting a particularly strong breakfast blend. When the tea was steeping, she whirled to face Franco. "I just realized...you've been here this whole time. Your job..."

He shrugged, seemingly at ease. "The only person who could fire me is, well...me. But I've been working."

"Francisco, I'm so sorry."

"Call me Franco. That's what my friends call me. Well, and my family."

"Franco... I don't know. I like Francisco. It sounds very dramatic."

"Francisco is the name of someone who can dance and cook. I can't do either."

Juliette laughed as she poured tea, forgoing proper cups in favor of thick mugs.

"Should I be worried?" He blew on the surface of the hot liquid.

"About what?"

"I haven't heard anything from the Grand Master. Devon said that he'd contact me because I need to be offered membership."

"Oh. Of course. Right." Juliette turned away, blindly opening a cupboard to cover her reaction. She'd left Franco hanging. There was too much to do, too much to figure out.

Where the hell was Sebastian? He should have been here

days ago, and if he'd just show up, she could officially make him one of her councilors and force him to help her.

Devon. Devon could help you. He could be one of your councilors.

Ignoring that annoying inner voice, she closed the cupboard door, going instead to the pantry. "I'm sure you'll be hearing from the Grand Master soon. You should attend the Winter Gala."

"Attend a gala?"

"Yes. Otherwise you'd have to wait months for the next big event."

"A gala...like with tuxedos?"

"I'm sure we can find someone to loan you a tux."

"I'll rent one, if I have to."

"Rent one..." Juliette shook her head. "This isn't a rented-tux type of event."

Franco groaned. Juliette pulled out a few energy bars, which were the only readily available snacks in the pantry.

"Er, thanks." He looked dubiously at the brightly wrapped package.

"I should probably go grocery shopping."

"I'm not one to talk, since I'm absolute crap at responsible adult things like keeping a regular schedule and cooking, but you look like you haven't eaten or slept in days."

"Gee, thanks." Juliette refused to feel self-conscious. She distinctly remembered showering earlier in an effort to wake herself up, and she'd put these clothes on fresh afterwards.

"Can I, uh, would you like to...go out to lunch?"

"No, I'm in the middle of something."

"Oh. Okay." Franco dropped his head, studying the nutritional information on the back of the energy bar.

"Did you...were you asking me out?"

"Devon said that people still date. Members, I mean. That's why I asked, but if that was inappropriate—"

Juliette felt herself blush, both from pleasure that he'd asked her out and embarrassment at how she'd replied. "No, it's not inappropriate, and I'm sorry. I've just been so focused."

"Wait, I realize I implied that the only reason you'd say no is if it was inappropriate." He blinked owlishly and ran a hand through his hair, immediately looking rumpled. "I totally respect your right to just say no for whatever reason."

They stared at each other, awkward in each other's presence for the first time. Juliette hated that she was making this sweet, hapless guy feel bad.

"Franco, I like you. That's why I kissed you. I just can't go out to lunch today."

He smiled and Juliette forgot how tired she was, forgot how much work she had to do. His eyes lit up when he smiled.

"I'm glad," he said.

"What?" It wasn't the most intelligent reply, but she'd lost the thread of the conversation.

"You said you liked me, and I said I'm glad." Franco tipped his head as he studied he, then picked up his phone.

Juliette waited for a minute but he kept his head down. Miffed, she said, "I have to get back to work."

"Lunch should be here in forty-five minutes." He set down the phone. "I hope you like Indian food."

"Food?"

"Yep. All hail GrubHub."

"I...actually Indian food sounds really good." It was nice to have someone just make a decision.

"And I've got my tablet with me, so I'll stay and work."

"You can't. What I'm working on is confidential."

"I'll stay in here, or in some other room." He slid off his stool and came over, crowding her against the counter. "I know what it's like to focus on something so much that you forget everything else. That's when you need someone to provide food and beverage."

"I'll be fine."

He cupped her face, thumbs rubbing her cheeks. His eyes were bright blue in the afternoon light. "I'm not saying you won't be. But I'm still going to take care of you."

Juliette closed her eyes, letting the weight of her head rest in his hands. "Thank you."

"You're welcome. Where is it safe for me to sit?"

Juliette took him to the small library, which had two desks, a long leather couch, and floor-to-ceiling bookcases. On the way, Franco grabbed his bag from the coat closet where he'd stashed it.

"Before I forget, I brought something you should look at." He pulled a small wooden box from his bag. "This was my grandfather's. The story, which is apparently true, was that the secret society gave him the box for safekeeping. He never opened it because he thought it was a test—if he didn't open it, they'd know he could resist temptation and keep a secret. It got shoved into a dresser along with all his other stuff. I hadn't thought about it in years until you showed up."

Juliette peered at the box. The top was carved with the triquetra. She reached for it but Franco pulled it back, setting it on the desk.

"Teasing me?"

"No. I'm making sure you don't get distracted from whatever you were working on."

Work—the piles and piles of member files in the other room. She should get back to it. Every second those files were outside the headquarters was a risk. She'd only brought the ones for unmatched members, and there was nothing incriminating—such as a description of the trinity—in these files. If an outsider were to walk in and find them, they wouldn't learn about the Trinity Masters, but they would certainly have a lot of questions as to why Juliette had that kind of information about so many different people.

She should get back to it.

Juliette slid down onto the couch, stifling a yawn. "What are you working on?"

"Transcribing some old letters. I finished scanning them before I got on the plane. Between the handwriting and the fading, it's taking an annoyingly long time."

Juliette rested her head on the arm of the couch. "What kind of letters are they?"

"...hoping to better understand the relationship between the families." Franco finished his explanation, zooming out until the entire page of the letter was visible.

Juliette didn't respond.

He twisted in his chair, not surprised to see her asleep. She was curled into a ball with her head on the edge of the couch. Her hands were tucked into the sleeves of her sweatshirt.

She looked small, vulnerable and exhausted. Even he wasn't dumb enough to say this, but she looked terrible—there were bags under her eyes and her face looked thinner than before.

Tablet in one hand, he sat on the couch then tugged Juliette's shoulders until she was lying flat, head on his lap. He brushed her hair back from her face, hoping this wasn't a completely creepy thing to do.

Normally *he* was the one strung out and exhausted-looking as a result of getting wrapped up in his work. It felt good to be on the other side of that equation, to be the one taking care instead of being cared for. Laying one hand protectively on her shoulder, Franco was content to simply be with her as she slept.

CHAPTER NINE

"I'm so full." Juliette wiped her fingers on a napkin, resisting the urge to lick them clean. "This is seriously some of the best food I've had in a long time."

"I'm glad you enjoyed it, I spent hours cooking it." Franco motioned vaguely to the microwave, where he'd reheated the food that had been delivered earlier while she slept.

"I expect nothing less from a man named Francisco."

He laughed. Her own chuckle turned into a massive yawn.

"You should go to bed." He adjusted his glasses, which had a tendency to slide down his nose.

Juliette eyed him. Where had this commanding tone come from? And why did she find it so appealing? "I slept all day."

"Not to be rude, but you still look tired."

"A gentleman never tells a lady when she looks poorly."

"I'm a terrible gentleman. Ask my mother. She gave up on me after she found a moldy bowl of cereal under my bed."

"Eww, teenagers are gross."

"Uh, that was when I was twenty-four and home from grad school for a visit."

"That's just sad." Juliette was ready to tease him more, but she yawned so widely that her jaw cracked.

"Come on." Franco rose and offered his hand.

She stared at his fingers, gripped by the strange feeling that if she took his hand, everything would change. If this were a movie there would be dramatic music playing. "Why do I feel so comfortable with you?"

"I feel the same way with you." His face was serious, sculpted lips pressed together in a thin line. "I feel like...maybe I've been waiting for you, for the Trinity Masters."

Juliette placed her fingers in his. "And maybe we've been waiting for you."

The atmosphere shifted. This was no longer about sleep; it was about the chemistry between them, desire that could no longer be denied.

Franco pulled her to her feet, brushing his hand down her back. Juliette guided them up the stairs, lacing her fingers with his. Her heart beat louder with each step they ascended.

She paused outside the bedroom door. "I need to say something."

Franco's heavy-lidded gaze traveled over her. "I want you."

"I want you, too, but—"

He detangled his fingers from hers, pointedly looking away. "Let me finish. Devon explained that members don't have serious relationships. I want you, but you aren't a casual-relationship kind of girl."

Juliette reached up and stroked his face. He said he wasn't a gentleman, but he was.

Good thing she didn't intend to behave like a lady.

"I'm not a girl, Franco. I'm a woman. A woman who knows what she wants and can handle the consequences."

She kissed him. This wasn't a soft or gentle kiss; it was a

kiss with intent. The intent to seduce, the intent to start something that could only end in sex.

Franco held back for a moment—either surprised or gentlemanly instincts at play—but then he returned the kiss, with interest.

He backed her up against the wall. Juliette hummed her approval as he tangled his fingers in her hair, tugging until she tipped her chin up. He trailed kisses down her jawline to her neck. She hooked one leg around his waist and he accepted her invitation, cupping her ass.

She would have given anything to be dressed in something sexier than leggings and a sweatshirt. Franco's hands slid under her top, the brush of his fingers on her bare skin making her shiver. She stopped worrying about what she was wearing.

"Bed," she whispered.

"Where?"

"In the bedroom."

Franco lifted his head from her neck. "I deserve that. Okay, smartass, where's the bedroom?"

Juliette suppressed a giggle. Wasn't there some saying about how laughter ruined sex? She leaned right and turned the doorknob.

"Nice." Franco cupped her ass with both hands. Juliette wrapped her arms and legs around him, kissing his neck as he carried her.

He made it three steps, tripped, and nearly dropped her.

Juliette yelped and managed to reach out and grab the doorframe while simultaneously dropping her feet to the floor. Franco tried to recover from the stumble, failed, and fell onto a pile of clothes on her floor. His glasses came off and skittered away.

Juliette stared at him sprawled on the ground, head and shoulders buried in a pile of clothes that needed to be dry-cleaned. A giggle burst from her lips. She slapped a hand over her mouth.

"Stop laughing." His voice was muffled and he made no attempt to move.

"I'm not laughing," she lied.

Franco rolled onto his back. His expression was a mix of sheepish and resigned.

"At least this time you didn't knock me down."

Franco got to his feet, looking around her room. His brows rose as he took in the piles of clothes and stacks of bins.

"This is what I was going to tell you—my room is a bit of a mess."

"Do you live out of plastic bins?"

"I don't really live here." The interlude hadn't cooled her desire, only muted it. "But that's not what I want to talk about."

Franco must have heard the change in her tone. He looked over in time to see her strip off her sweatshirt. Her bra wasn't fancy, but based on Franco's reaction it didn't matter.

He reached for her but Juliette danced back out of his reach. "Nuh-uh. You next. Take off your shirt."

Franco stripped off everything above the waist. He had nice pecs and a flat stomach. A line of dark hair trailed from his bellybutton to the waistband of his pants.

Juliette stripped off her socks and Franco mirrored her action, removing his shoes and socks. When she reached for her leggings, he stopped her.

"No, let me."

He ran one finger up her arm, across her shoulder and then down her sternum. She shivered when his finger slid over her abdomen. When he finally reached for her pants, Juliette had to fight the urge to grab him and force him to move faster.

Franco dropped to his knees then used both hands to slide her leggings and underwear down.

It was shocking and arousing to be exposed before him, especially because his mouth was so close to her sex. She was wet and throbbing, ready for his hands, mouth and cock.

When the fabric pooled around her ankles she kicked it away. Franco ran his hands up the outside of her legs. Cupping her hipbones in his palms, he rubbed his thumbs along the line of her pubic hair.

Juliette tangled her fingers in his hair and gently tugged, asking without words for him to do more, take more.

When he pressed against the inside of her knees, she spread her legs.

"Tell me what you like," he said. Then his fingers were on her, in her. He stroked the seam of her sex then dipped his thumb in. Juliette gasped, throwing her head back.

His thumb settled on her clit, rubbing in small, hard circles. Arousal shifted from a slow burn to a fiery need, the kind of desire that could not be denied or ignored.

"Put your fingers in me," she demanded. "Please," she begged.

"Tell me you want me."

"I want you. I want you." His thumb continued the maddening circles over her clit. The orgasm was building—each moment, each movement, ratcheting it tighter inside her.

"You're wet; very wet."

"I need you in me."

"And I need to be in you. But first I want to see you come."

Franco slid one finger into her. Juliette's body clamped down, the pleasure both startling and long-awaited.

"More," she pleaded.

In response, he pressed a second finger deep inside then removed his thumb from her clit. She was about to protest when he dipped his head down, fastening his mouth over the bundle of nerves. His tongue was at first softer than his fingers, but when he started to flick her clit, the sensations were hard and sharp.

He pulled back to take a deep breath. "I can feel you clenching around my fingers."

"Either finish me now or get on the bed and fuck me."

"I'd planned to keep you like this, *querida*." His thumb returned to her clit, this time circling. The touch was enough to keep her on edge, but not enough to give her the sweet release she needed. "Take off your bra." His voice was rich and dark.

Juliette released his hair and stripped off her last piece of clothing. Her nipples were hard. Even the whisper of air from the heating system was enough to have her moaning and licking her lips.

"Touch them."

Juliette closed her eyes and obeyed. In the darkness behind her lids, the world was full of mellow, rich colors and the warm sound of his voice. She cupped and massaged her breasts before lightly pinching her nipples.

"Harder," he demanded.

She could feel him watching her, knew from his tone that the sight of her playing with her own breasts was arousing him.

Opening her eyes, she watched him as she pulled hard on her nipples, hard enough that she gasped and moaned. Franco's gaze went from her breasts to her face and back again. He was dark and intense. Focused. As if she were the only woman in the world.

Devon.

Unbidden, an image of Devon flashed through her mind. He was the only other one who'd looked at her with that level of intensity. The memory of his touch, his expression as he slid into her, the sound of his breath in her ear as he came, flooded her consciousness. Rather than detract from her current experience the memory enhanced it, notching her desire up another level.

Her legs started to shake. Juliette had to brace her hands on Franco. Guilt lanced through her when she looked down at him—she shouldn't be thinking about Devon right now.

"Bed." Franco rolled to his feet and started shucking his pants. Juliette threw the messy covers onto the floor.

Franco's cock, once free of his pants, was a sight to behold. It was thick and dark, the foreskin already retracted, the head glistening.

She couldn't help but compare it to Devon's cock, which was longer and thinner. Guilt once more rolled through her.

Franco climbed on the bed and beckoned her to join him. Juliette pushed him down onto his back then straddled his hips. His cock lay on his belly, so she reached down, gently stroking the head as she tipped it up into position. She rubbed it against her pussy, back and forth through the wet valley of her body, moaning each time it brushed her clit.

Franco took one nipple in each hand, plucking and pulling on the tight pink nubs.

Juliette pressed his cock back until the head was nestled against her entrance. Franco cupped her rib cage, thumbs pressed against the underside of her breasts.

"Juliette." Her name was a demand and a prayer on his lips.

"Franco." Sliding her hand out of the way, Juliette lowered her hips.

His cock pressed into her. It had been a long time since she'd had sex, and his cock was thicker than anything she'd ever taken before. She paused, her pussy pulsing around the invader.

"Are you okay?"

"Yes, just getting used to it."

His brows drew together. "I don't want to hurt you."

"You won't." To prove it, Juliette sank down another inch. The head of his cock rubbed against her G spot, and Juliette had to briefly close her eyes as pleasure swept through her.

"Juliette, Juliette." Now Franco's eyes were closed, too, and she could see the tension in his shoulders and arms.

She sank down all the way, his cock seated fully within her. Taking a few slow breaths, she allowed herself to revel in the moment, to let it imprint on her. There was something magical, almost spiritual about this first moment of being joined with someone.

Rising until only the head of his cock was inside her, Juliette then slammed her hips down. The speed made it a totally different sensation. Her body spasmed around his cock, her pussy squeezing and releasing. Franco hissed out a breath, his fingers pressing into her skin.

With more intent than finesse, he dropped one hand down and wedged his thumb between their groins. As Juliette rocked her hips forward, Franco's thumb zeroed in on her clit.

The orgasm ripped through her, pleasure bright and sharp like a flash of white light. Her head fell back, her nails dug into Franco's chest and she screamed in pleasure.

"Don't stop," Franco demanded, but she was too lost in the orgasm to pay attention.

He sat up, hugged her to him, and rolled until she was on her back under him. Franco captured her lips in a hot, open-mouthed kiss as he kneed her legs farther apart and settled his cock back at the entrance to her sex.

When he thrust in, Juliette jerked her lips from his, letting out another cry of pleasure. She sank her nails into his back, clinging to Franco. Once more the memory of Devon rose in her mind. This time it wasn't guilt that flooded her, but more desire. Thinking of the man who had until so recently been her fiancé was heightening her pleasure.

"There's someone missing," she whispered. She was only vaguely aware of what she was saying.

Franco paused. "Someone?"

"Yes."

"I think—" He started thrusting in earnest, words puffs of air against her shoulder. "I think you're right."

Franco changed the angle of his thrust and Juliette yelped in pleasure, nails scoring Franco's back.

They were so lost in the moment that neither heard the footsteps.

The silence from Juliette was deafening. Devon strode up the few steps to the door of her shared house. He hadn't heard from her since she'd texted him about meeting with Franco days ago.

He'd reached out to Harrison, but the former Grand Master hadn't heard from Juliette either. He'd been keeping an eye on her, and knew she was going back and forth from home and the Boston Public Library—the Trinity Masters' headquarters.

Whatever she was doing when she was there, she was doing it alone. The only person she might have contacted was Sebastian, but Devon hadn't been able to get ahold of him either.

Devon used a copy of the key he'd had made years ago, which he'd sworn to use only for emergencies.

"Juliette?"

There was no answer. He checked the kitchen first. There were half-empty to-go boxes spread out on the island. At least she was eating.

The spot between his shoulder blades was itching—something was wrong.

Devon checked the living room, shocked by what he saw. There were files everywhere. After a moment of assessing, he realized there weren't actually that many—thirty in total, if he had to guess—but they were spread out all over the floor.

Stooping, he peered at the nearest one. His heart sank. These were the member files—exactly what he'd been afraid of.

As he straightened, Devon thought he heard something. He paused, but there was no other sound.

Careful not to touch anything, Devon moved through the room, checking the names on each file. He didn't find either his name or Sebastian's.

That didn't mean she hadn't seen them, didn't mean that she didn't know.

A noise again—this time he was *sure* he'd heard something. Something that sounded a lot like a scream.

Devon's heart stopped. Juliette.

Racing from the living room, he bounded up the stairs. The sound had come from too far away to have originated on the ground floor. One of the bedroom doors was open.

She cried out again, but this time it wasn't so much a scream as a moan. Devon's steps slowed. It sounded like...

Heart heavy, Devon stopped in the doorway.

The bed was in profile to the door, giving him a perfect side-on view of what was happening. Juliette lay on her back, hair spread around her head in a golden halo. As he watched, she arched her back, breasts brushing against Franco's chest.

He was surprisingly well muscled, his ass flexing as he pumped into Juliette.

Twin urges tore through Devon. He wanted to rip Franco away from Juliette and beat him to a bloody pulp. He also wanted to jump on the bed and join them. He'd never had the opportunity to have a *ménage a trois* with Juliette, but that was a matter of circumstance, not possessiveness.

Neither noticed him, and as Devon watched, Juliette whispered something to Franco, who bent his head, brushing his lips against Juliette's cheek as he replied.

That was what broke him—not jealousy of the physical act, but of the emotional connection they clearly shared.

A connection he'd once had, but lost.

"Juliette." He said her name without thinking. They hadn't seen him, so the right thing to do would be to walk away.

Franco reacted first. He looked over then froze. "Devon."

To the other man's credit, his first reaction was to drop the shoulder closest to the door, shielding Juliette's nudity with his body.

"Don't stop," Juliette moaned.

Devon's cock twitched in his pants. He knew that voice—that was the Juliette he loved and longed for, the girl who didn't hide her feelings or reactions. That voice belonged to the girl who danced in the Paris moonlight, not the girl who walked out on him at dawn.

"Uh, Devon's here. We need to, er, stop or something."

Juliette pushed on Franco's shoulder and turned her head. "I know Devon's here."

Their gazes met, and Devon had to grab either side of the doorframe to keep himself from entering the room and going to her. Juliette's eyes were shadowed, the pupils huge. Maybe it was just wishful thinking but he would have sworn that when she looked at him, fresh desire lit her expression.

Franco eased back and knelt, still between Juliette's splayed thighs. He looked around, muttering, "Need a blanket or something..."

Devon and Juliette maintained eye contact. Devon was waiting for her to tell him to leave. To sneer her derision. She didn't. It seemed that she, too, was waiting for something, but he didn't know what.

Franco slid off the bed and picked up a sheet. Juliette rolled on her side, facing Devon.

Franco stopped and looked between them. "This seems like a good time to ask what, exactly, the two of you's deal is."

"I lost my virginity to Devon." Juliette ran her hand over her bare hip.

"Juliette is my fiancée." Wood creaked under his fingers.

"Your fiancée?" Franco's eyes widened. "Uh…"

"No, I'm not. Devon was, from the day I was born until last week, my betrothed."

"Betrothed? I think I'm missing something."

Devon shook his head. "I can't, Juliette. I can't accept that we're over."

"The Grand Master has spoken." Juliette's hand trailed up her side until she lightly brushed her breast.

Devon wanted to respond, but he was too distracted by her nakedness, by the smell of sex that hung in the air.

"Franco." Juliette sat up, speaking to the other man while her gaze remained focused on Devon. "Do you remember when I said something was missing?"

Franco's gaze switched from Juliette to Devon. "You said someone. *Someone* was missing."

"And now he's here." Juliette shifted to her knees and motioned Franco to join her on the bed. Cautiously, he did, positioning himself behind Juliette.

"Devon, take off your clothes."

Run. Run like hell because if you don't, this is just going to make the heartbreak that much worse.

Maybe he wasn't as smart as he thought he was, because Devon stepped through the doorway and started unbuttoning his shirt.

CHAPTER TEN

Franco was tentative at first, hands resting on her hips then rubbing circles over her abdomen as he and Juliette watched Devon undress. She could practically feel his confusion and need to ask questions, but he smartly said nothing. What was between her and Devon was so complicated that truly explaining it would have been a death sentence to the moment they were living in. She wasn't ready to face reality. She wanted to revel in the arousal and desire that made her brave and reckless.

Juliette felt powerful and free. She wanted these men, and she was going to have them. There were no restrictions, no reasons why she couldn't be with them. For the first time in her life she got to behave the way other members did—taking her pleasure when and how she wanted it.

"Do you want to do this?" she asked Franco.

"I'm not exactly sure how this works, but I think so." The rich, dark voice he used when he was really aroused was gone, replaced by his normal slightly bemused tone, but Juliette was sure she could get him revved up again. One down, one to go.

Devon was no stranger to the idea of a *ménage*, but they'd both grown up anticipating a sex life with two women, not two men.

When he finally shed the last of his clothing, Juliette was pleasantly surprised to see that Devon was already hard. Two down.

Franco's hands paused mid-motion.

"You okay?" she asked him again.

"Yes. I am." His voice had changed again. When his hands resumed their caress it was with more intent and intensity. It seemed that she wasn't going to have to coax Franco into enjoying this. He was as into the sight of a naked Devon as she was. Devon was pale, like a cream marble statue, his skin contrasting with his warm brown hair.

He paused, hands flexing at his sides, gaze traveling over Juliette and Franco. He seemed to be waiting, as if he wasn't sure what to do next.

"Devon."

Saying his name seemed to free him from his indecision. He came to the side of the bed, but made no move to join them. Juliette knee-walked across the mattress until she could reach him. His body was both familiar and strange. It was the first time she'd touched him without the pressure of their betrothal weighing her down.

"We're not in Paris." She put her hands on his chest, splaying her fingers.

"No, we're not."

"And we're not betrothed."

Devon closed his eyes. "Juliette, please. Don't."

"Don't do this?" She dropped one hand onto his hard cock, running her fingers along the sensitive underside.

He didn't respond except to moan.

"Franco." Juliette reached her free hand back, urging him

to join them, creating a bridge between the men, uniting the three of them together.

With an increasing enthusiasm she hadn't dared hope for, Franco knelt behind her, his legs on either side of hers. His warm chest pressed against her and his cock nestled in the small of her back. He brushed her hair aside and started kissing her neck.

Juliette licked her lips. "Franco, I want you to play with my pussy." The graphic words were hot on her tongue, but they didn't embarrass her. She found giving orders unexpectedly arousing.

Without hesitation, Franco's hands slid from her belly button down to her sex, which was open and exposed between her splayed thighs. He spread the lips of her pussy, letting the air invade and cool her most intimate parts. She moaned her approval.

"Devon," she panted. "I want you to play with my breasts and kiss me."

Devon took his time, brushing her hair back from her face and massaging her shoulders before sliding his hands to her breasts. He rolled her nipples against his flat palms, a delicate yet intense sensation. Her body remembered his unique touch and responded accordingly.

Devon kissed her—a sweet, closed-mouth kiss. That wasn't what she wanted or needed. Taking his cock in her hands, Juliette stroked him the way he liked, the way he'd taught her to. She knew the instant he stopped thinking and questioning and gave in to the desire that emanated from his body like heat. He growled low in his throat and deepened the kiss. It was almost punishing in its ferocity.

Juliette squeezed his cock and nipped his tongue. They battled for control of the kiss, two well-matched opponents who'd been fighting this war for a long time.

Franco was her undoing. He responded to the increased intensity in the room by pressing two fingers inside Juliette while also pinching her clit with his other hand.

Gasping in pleasure, Juliette broke the kiss, tipping her head back. It was a base, animalistic surrender. She exposed her throat to Devon and he took advantage, nipping the side of her neck Franco wasn't already kissing.

Devon pressed his lips to her ear. "You're mine. You'll always be mine, and I'll always be yours."

She didn't have time to react to his words, because Devon did something completely unexpected.

He cupped Franco's chin, lifted the other man's head, and kissed him.

Juliette slid out from between the two men, watching carefully. "Oh that's hot."

Franco was tense, his body angled and stiff as he kept himself away from Devon except for where their lips were fused. Franco's eyes were wide, but when Devon changed the angle of the kiss, they closed.

Despite Franco's awkward posture, the sight was intensely arousing. Both men were gorgeous in their own ways—Devon familiar and classically handsome, Franco dramatic and alluring with his dark hair and blue eyes.

Franco relaxed, shifting until there was only a handspan of space between them. Juliette laid a hand on each of their shoulders. As one they turned to her. Juliette kissed Franco first, and with his taste still on her lips, turned to kiss Devon.

She let her hands roam over their chests and shoulders. With her eyes closed, she couldn't be sure who was plucking her nipples or stroking her pussy.

"I need more."

"Turn around," Devon ordered. "I'm going to fuck you while you suck Franco's cock."

Juliette spun, planting her knees near the edge of the bed, spreading her legs to give Devon access. Without waiting, he slid into her. She was ready for him, slick with wetness from having Franco fuck her. Devon's long cock pressed inside, each glorious inch filling her a bit more. Franco lay on his side, hesitantly inching his hips towards her. Bracing herself on one elbow, she grabbed his cock, tugging lightly so he would scoot closer. When his hips were in position, Juliette braced her forearm on his belly, fist around the base of Franco's cock. She wrapped her lips around the glands, and when Devon thrust she lowered her head, taking Franco's cock deep into her mouth.

Franco reached under her, plucking and tugging her nipples. Sensation came at her from all sides—Devon's cock in her pussy, Franco's fingers on her nipples and cock in her mouth.

Devon gathered up her hair, pulling it just hard enough that her scalp tingled. He knew her, knew how to push her over the edge. Juliette screamed around Franco's cock as she came. Devon slammed into her, thrusting hard and fast as he, too, orgasmed.

Without giving her time to gather herself, Devon pulled out and rolled her onto her back.

"Fuck her," he told Franco.

Franco once more slid into place between her legs, dark brows lowered, gaze intense. Devon, still breathing hard from his orgasm, stretched out beside her. He cupped her breast, angling her nipple so he could suck it as Franco fucked her.

Juliette's head thrashed on the pillow. She was going to come again. Franco's stomach was slick with sweat as he fucked her, the taste of his cock still on her tongue.

Devon pinched her nipple with his fingers, kissing his way

along her side until he found her mouth, tasting Franco, whose breath washed over both of them.

"I'm close. Please." Juliette clung to Franco's tensed arm with one hand, the other buried in Devon's hair.

Devon slid one hand down her torso until he buried his fingers in her pussy. He stroked the entrance to her body, where Franco's cock slid in and out, then pressed down on her clit, rubbing it against her pelvic bone.

Juliette screamed as she came again. This time the sound wasn't muffled. There was no hiding the intensity of her pleasure.

Franco groaned as he came.

Devon tugged her out from under Franco then made sure they were each safely positioned on the too-small-for-three-people bed.

The heat woke her. Juliette opened her eyes but didn't feel fully awake. This was a dream. She was staring at a man's shoulder, while another's arm was draped across her waist. Breathing slow and deep, she waited for the dream to fade, waited for reality to return.

But this *was* real. She was lying in the middle between the two men, both of whom were radiating heat.

Juliette eased Devon's arm off her then inched her way down to the bottom of the bed. Pale sunlight haloed the curtains, just enough illumination that she could make her way to the door.

"Don't you dare."

She turned to see Devon awake and propped on one elbow. "What?"

His face was an oval of pale skin in the muted darkness. "Don't you dare leave. You always leave."

Juliette turned away, though she doubted he could see her expression. "I'm just going to the bathroom."

"No, you're not." He got out of bed.

Juliette slid out of the bedroom, heart beating with the rapid pace of a rabbit fleeing a fox. He followed her, six feet of naked intent.

Last night had been...she couldn't believe it. She'd never been so bold or sure of herself as she had been when she'd orchestrated that *ménage*.

But the truly terrifying part was how right it had felt...and how much she wanted it to happen again. She'd woken assuming it was a dream—the kind that was too good to be true. But what frustrated her was that now, when she had the power to walk away from Devon, she couldn't seem to do it.

"You're shutting down, locking me out." He stalked her, radiating frustration. "Do you know how much I hate dawn in Paris?"

"You hate dawn in Paris?" Juliette shook her head. "That's a ridiculous thing to say."

"Is it?" His voice was raw with anger. "Last night was amazing, and yet here we are—you treating me like enemy number one."

"I'm not—" Juliette bit back the denial. It would have been a lie. He deserved better than that. "I'm sorry." She took a deep breath. "You're right, last night *was* amazing."

"And what does it mean?"

"Mean? It doesn't mean anything. We're all unattached adults who chose to have a good time."

"Damn it, Juliette. Don't. Please."

"Don't what, Devon? Tell me what you want me to say." Emotion made her throat tight even as her fingers tingled with the need to touch him.

"I want you to say that you'll reinstate our trinity. I want you to say that I *mean* something to you."

The emotion in his voice made her breath catch. Her voice

was soft when she answered. "Of course you mean something to me."

"Really? Because at the first chance you got, you tossed me aside."

"No, Devon, I didn't." She lived in shades of gray, and he was speaking in black and white. "You have no problem with how we grew up, or with the arranged marriage, but guess what? I do. I idolized you, loved you." Embarrassment at the memory of how she'd fawned on him, how desperately she'd wanted his attention, clawed at her.

"What happened? What did I do to make you hate me?"

"I don't hate you. I could never hate you." It would be easier if she did. "But I've never been in control of my life or my feelings. I had no choice but to love you."

"That's not true." He sounded exasperated.

"Really? I grew up living in half of a fairy tale—the princesses betrothed to the handsome prince." Still naked, she mock-curtseyed, anger bitter on her tongue. "But in *my* story there's another princess, and whoops, before we could get married and live happily ever after, I grew up and got an education. I realized that whatever feelings you and I have for one another aren't organic, they're manufactured by circumstance."

"My feelings for you are real."

"How the hell would you know, Devon?" She was yelling. She couldn't stop herself. "You never questioned any of this, and when I started to you shut me down. The first time I tried to talk to you about how barbaric some of the Trinity Masters' practices are you basically patted me on the head and dismissed me."

Devon was shaking his head. "I don't remember it like that."

"Of course you don't. Why would you? For you it was nothing, a throw-away conversation. For me..." Juliette felt suddenly weary. She went to the head of the stairs, descending a few steps so she could take a seat. "For me, that was the moment I realized that I mattered less to you than the Trinity Masters, and I always will."

"That's not true."

"Spare me." She rubbed her palms on her shins, curling into a ball for warmth. "I don't have time for this. I have work to do."

Devon didn't respond, so she looked up. He had the heels of his hands pressed into his eye sockets. When he dropped his arms his face was haunted.

"Why didn't you tell me how you felt?"

She shrugged. "Because my feelings didn't matter."

"Of course—"

"No, Devon. They didn't. I joined the instant I turned eighteen with no idea what I was really committing to. My trinity was set. The fact that I grew up and started to see the flaws in our practices and resent everyone who didn't share my feelings," she motioned to him, "that's *my* problem. And until now, there was not a damn thing I could do about it."

Devon joined her on the steps. "My feelings for you haven't changed."

"Don't you get it? They aren't real." Juliette swiped a hand angrily through the air and blinked back tears. "You never had any real choice."

"You're wrong." Hard lines bracketed his mouth as he grimaced. "If that were true, I would have the same feelings for Rose that I do for you, but I don't."

"What?"

He cupped her face. "I love you, Juliette. Not Rose, not the Trinity Masters. I love *you*, and every time you walked away from me it broke my heart."

"You don't love me." Her throat was tight. He couldn't love

her, because if he did it would make it so much harder to pretend she didn't still love him. And she had gotten very good at pretending.

"Of course I do. I'm just not good at showing it. I was afraid." He leaned forward and laid his head against hers. "I'm still afraid."

In that moment, she realized he wasn't the pillar of strength and duty she always assumed. He seemed weary and vulnerable. Juliette wrapped her arms around his shoulders, overcome by the need to comfort and protect him.

"There are things I needed—need—to tell you." His voice was soft in her ear. "Those things prevented me from being completely honest with you, and when you started to act like you hated me..."

"I've never hated you. I wish I had, wish I did."

"Don't leave me, Jules."

It was an old nickname, one he'd stopped using after that first meeting in Paris. She'd taken it as a sign that he now saw her as an adult, as a woman. It brought tears to her eyes, the way a familiar smell from a childhood home could.

She was saved from responding by Franco, who'd approached unnoticed and was holding a buzzing cell phone.

"Uh, someone's phone keeps ringing."

Devon glared at Franco, but then stood and took his phone. Franco murmured that he was sorry for interrupting. Devon looked at the screen, and in an instant the raw emotion etched on his face was hidden under his normal stoic expression.

"I have to take this." He disappeared into the bedroom.

Franco hesitated then took a seat beside Juliette on the steps. He was dressed, but as he sat he stripped off his shirt and handed it to Juliette, who pulled it on.

"So you and Devon..."

Juliette huddled in on herself, weary from lack of sleep and emotional upheaval. She was still reeling from her conversation with Devon, so she answered Franco without much forethought.

"Devon and I were part of a trinity, along with a woman named Rose Hancock. Our families have been members since the beginning. My father decided it was time to unite the Adamses, Ashers and Hancocks."

"Your father? I thought the Grand Master picked the trinities."

"He does." Juliette turned her head to stare at Franco.

"Oh. Ohhhh." Franco nodded as he put it together. "That explains why you were the one sent to find me."

"Actually, my father didn't send me, because he's dead."

"I'm sorry." Franco stroked her shoulder.

"It was a long time ago. He died before I was old enough to realize how twisted my upbringing was because of the choices he made for me."

"If it wasn't your father, who is the Grand Master?"

"The Grand Master's identity is a secret to most people. They have a council they work with. Who the councilors are is also a secret."

"Lots of secrets."

"Yes." She was fighting the urge to tell Franco who she was, to confide in him. He was a good listener, and he'd shown that, when needed, he could step up and take charge. He would be a good councilor, despite the fact that he knew nothing about the Trinity Masters.

Before she could decide what, if anything, to tell him, Devon emerged from the bedroom. He was fully dressed and his face was set in hard lines. "I have to go."

Juliette nodded once, but didn't look at him.

"Jules, I don't *want* to go." He grabbed her by the arms and hauled her up, forcing her to meet his gaze. "We're not done.

Not done with this conversation and not done with our relationship."

She struggled under the weight of his complete focus. It still made her feel like the most important woman in the world. She tried to remind herself that she bowed to no one anymore. She could walk away. "That's not your decision to make. It's the Grand Master's."

"Then I'll beg." He kissed her hard and deep, leaving her breathless. "I'll refuse any other *ménage*. I'd rather be expelled from the Trinity Masters than give up."

He kissed her again, with enough force and intent that her head fell back. It was a *Gone with the Wind* kiss, but instead of anger it tasted of desperation. "Juliette Adams, I love you. I always have, and I always will. Don't forget that."

Then he was gone, taking the stairs two at a time while looking at his phone. The door opened then closed.

"You two have issues."

Juliette looked at Franco, who was shaking his head ruefully. She burst out laughing.

"Yes, we do." Juliette held out her hand. "I think it's time you saw the Trinity Masters' headquarters."

Franco took her hand and climbed to his feet. "Further down the rabbit hole. Excellent."

The Boston Public Library grand hallway had an elegant arched and illustrated roof, stone floors and the kind of echoing sense of history that all great buildings developed over time. It was surprisingly busy, though the noise level was a library-appropriate hush. Franco wanted to stop at the desk and speak to the librarians, to explore the stacks, but Juliette was forging ahead. Promising himself a return visit, he followed her to the elevator. They went to the top floor then snaked their way through several hallways, Juliette leading the way while toting a duffle bag. He was carrying his grandfather's wood box.

By the time they reached the rare-book room, they were alone. A keypad protected the locked door. Juliette paused then stepped back. "You do it."

"Me?"

"Yes. The code is three, three, three."

"That's easy to remember. And appropriate."

The lock clicked and he opened the door, motioning Juliette to precede him in.

"Make sure you close it behind you."

Franco shut the door, but if Juliette said anything else he didn't hear it. The rare-book room was the stuff of his dreams. Tables supplied with boxes of cotton gloves begged visitors to select one of the carefully archived books and open them, revealing the secrets inside. Each shelf had a small plaque with the subject engraved on it. He gravitated towards one with diaries that had belonged to members of the semi-secret Masonic Temple.

"Franco... Franco... Francisco!"

"Huh?"

"You're mumbling to yourself." Juliette was fighting back a smile.

"This is fantastic. What an amazing collection. Who's the lead curator?"

"The books are not why we're here."

Franco gasped like an actor in a soap opera. "Bite your tongue, woman. The books are always why we're here."

"I promise, what I'm about to show you is more interesting than these."

"Impossible."

"Really?" She motioned to a section of wall. He stepped closer and discovered a triquetra inscribed into the plaster. Below the symbol were three words. "*Mitimur in Vetitum.*"

"I didn't take Latin," he said.

"It translates to 'We strive for the forbidden'." Juliette set down her bag, placed both hands on the symbol and pushed. A door-size section of wall popped in, and then slid to the side, disappearing into a pocket in the wall.

"Come on." Juliette stepped into the small, dark space. Franco joined her. The door closed behind them, sealing them in total darkness.

Before he had time to seriously start to worry, a light clicked on.

The room was as small as a closet and rather unremarkable, with walls of paneled wood, the floor the same carpet as the outer room.

"Usually whoever helped recruit you would bring you in the first time. After that, if you need to come here, you'll get a letter from the Grand Master. Usually the letter will have a box number on it." She motioned to the wood paneling. There were numbers etched into the wood, seemingly at random.

Juliette pressed her finger against a number. A small section of paneling popped open.

"What would be inside?"

"Usually more instructions or a key."

"And the note would have instructions for the next place to go, like a treasure hunt?"

"Not quite." Juliette pushed on the side of the back wall and yet another hidden door opened, revealing a narrow elevator.

"A secret elevator?"

She hit the single call button. "Yes." Once they were inside, the elevator descended automatically.

"We're going down." Franco tried to keep his voice calm, but a mixture of excitement and fear made it hard to keep his cool.

"To the subbasement."

The elevator door opened and a long, wide marble hallway stretched out in front of them. Columns supported the high-arched ceiling, which mimicked the grand hallway above.

"Welcome to the home of the Trinity Masters."

Franco's footsteps echoed endlessly off the stone as he followed her into the belly of the beast.

"No one knows this is here?"

"Only members."

"But surely the library staff realize?"

"The head of the library and many of the senior staff, as well as most of the board of trustees, are members. The Trinity Masters helped construct the library."

Midway down the hall were openings in the walls, one to the right, another to the left. Juliette pointed to the left hall.

"Normally when you're here, you need to wear a robe. Down here are changing rooms. The robes are inside."

"Do I need to change now?"

"I'm not…maybe." Juliette looked unsure. "Yes, you should. I'll show you." She guided him to an elegant, dark-wood door.

"What's in the other hall?" he asked curiously.

"Private changing rooms, but those ones are connected to the medallion room. When people are called to the altar, that's where they go."

The main changing room looked like the kind of thing that would exist in a luxury spa. There were full-length lockers, padded benches and recessed lighting. An archway led to a tiled room full of private showers.

Each locker had a small plaque on the door with a measurement on it.

"What's this?" He pointed to the number.

"Sadly, it's nothing mysterious. It's just the size of the robe inside. Sixty means sixty inches, which is the size robe you'd need."

He opened the locker, whistling as he fingered the heavy velvet robe.

"I need to do something." Juliette took the box he'd brought and stuffed it into the duffle, then hefted her bag back onto her shoulder as he stored his jacket and sweater. "You can leave your clothes on this time."

"This time?"

"Some of the ceremonies require people to be naked, so usually everyone just strips before putting their robes on."

"Naked. Right."

"Don't worry so much."

"Worry? Me? I'm just in a super-secret underground temple-thing with a woman I've only known for a week."

"Aw, now you're hurting my feelings. It's been nearly two weeks."

"Considering how much has already happened I'm a bit scared to think what my life will be like in another two weeks."

He'd meant it as a joke, but Juliette's features creased with worry.

Robe hanging off his shoulders but not yet closed, Franco rubbed her arms. "I was kidding."

"Are you really sure you want to do this?"

"What I said before, that I'd been waiting for you, for this... it's true. I'm ready for this. Though I'm not sure what this is. What are we doing here? Is the Grand Master here?"

"Yes. That's why we came. Sorry, I'm not great at this new member induction thing, since I didn't go through it. Normally there would be a lot of hoops you'd need to jump through, and a mandatory waiting period, but you're a special circumstance."

With that Juliette slipped out, leaving Franco to practice not freaking out. When she returned she held a note-card sized envelope made of paper so thick it felt like fabric.

Francisco,

If you are ready to take your place among the members of the Trinity Masters join me in the altar room. If you choose not to join, you must never speak about the Trinity Masters again, nor wear your grandfather's ring in public. Failure to maintain silence about us will result in repercussions.

Grand Master

"Yikes."

"You can leave."

"No...I want to stay."

"Even after last night?"

"Especially after last night. I know things are complicated for you and Devon, but what we had, the three of us, felt special."

"It *was* special." She sighed and relaxed, smiling slightly. "Once you're done, take the hall all the way to the end. There are three doors. Take the center one. That leads to the grand hall, which has the altar."

"Altar? As in the sacrificial kind?"

"If you're ready to join, it's time to make it official." She squeezed his hand. "I'll see you when it's over?"

After a week of waiting, he should have been ready for this moment, but it suddenly seemed to be happening way too fast. "What do I have to do?"

"Don't worry, the Grand Master will tell you."

CHAPTER ELEVEN

Francisco stood on one side of a large stone altar, trembling hands hidden under the sleeves of his robe. He was shivering from the cold. This far underground, with unforgiving stone rooms and high ceilings, the chill was creeping through his skin and settling in his bones.

Who was he kidding? It might be cold, but it was nerves that caused the tremor. He'd told Juliette he was ready, but it wasn't until this moment that he truly accepted the gravity of what he was about to do.

Standing across from him was a slight figure in a black robe. The Grand Master.

A heavy gold chain hung from the Grand Master's shoulders. The robe completely concealed the person's identity and added a menacing note to the whole event. This scene would not be out of place in a horror movie—if that robe concealed a demon instead of a powerful human. That absurd thought was enough to shake him out of his anticipatory paralysis. Franco took a deep breath and squared his shoulders. He was ready.

"Francisco Garcia Santiago, do you understand the rules

and privileges of the Trinity Masters?" The voice was gravelly, but strange sounding, as if the person were artificially lowering their voice.

"I do."

"You will live by our laws and rules, dedicate yourself to both the United States of America and the protection of the Trinity Masters."

"I will."

"You will marry in the secret way of the Trinity Masters, accepting two others into your life, and protect them and the secret of your trinity, placing them above all others."

"Quick question, can I, uh, tell you my preferences? I mean, maybe you'd appreciate some suggestions?"

Silence.

Franco shifted. "Sorry, forget I said anything. What was the question again?"

"You will marry in the secret way of the Trinity Masters, accepting two others into your life, and protect them and the secret of your trinity, placing them above all others in your life."

The Grand Master's voice had lost some of its gravelly quality, and there was a distinct note of exasperation. Strange, it almost sounded like…

"I will." He rushed the words, wanting to make sure the Grand Master knew that he was committed.

"Francisco Garcia Santiago, lost legacy to our order, welcome to the Trinity Masters." The Grand Master extended a gloved hand, placing it on the altar. When it pulled back, a gold ring awaited.

Franco picked it up and slid it on his finger. It was nearly identical to his grandfather's, but the gold was shiny and new.

"Thank you, Grand Master." Franco dipped his head in a small bow.

When he looked up, the Grand Master was gone.

Juliette was waiting for him in the locker room. She'd had to rush to shed the Grand Master's robe and chain and make it back here before Franco did. Luckily she was familiar with the network of halls and secret doors that connected the smaller and less public areas of the headquarters.

"Did you join?" she asked him when he entered.

Franco held up his hand and grinned, showing off his ring.

She answered his smile with one of her own. "I'm glad." That was certainly the truth.

"I may have done something stupid."

"Uh-oh, what did you do?"

"I asked the Grand Master if I could help pick my trinity."

"Oops." Juliette forced herself to wince rather than sigh in exasperation. In the ceremony, she'd had to fight the urge to take off her shoe and smack him upside the head with it.

Juliette was trying to imagine how her father or Harrison would have handled the situation. Hopefully intimidating silence was appropriate. Considering how strong-willed most of the members were, it couldn't be the first time someone had said something like that, or asked if they could have some input into their trinity. The awkward way Franco had done it was uniquely him. She wanted to both hug him and smack him.

And that was one of the reasons she was starting to have feelings for him. Very serious feelings for him.

Franco took a seat on the bench beside her. He carefully picked up one of her hands in his.

"Juliette, I need to ask you something."

His blue eyes searched her face, and Juliette's stomach tightened. *Shit.*

"Are you the Grand Master?"

"Dead. He should be dead. Have him murdered."

Juliette looked up from her stack of papers. Franco was sitting cross-legged on the floor of the Grand Master's office sorting through files. His hair was standing up from where he'd run his hands through it. His glasses were on crooked and he was still half-wearing the robe, which was now rumpled. He looked somewhat crazy.

When she'd admitted to him that she was the Grand Master, her primary feeling had been relief. Because he was so new, Franco had been impressed and interested, but not completely intimidated or shocked. That's what she needed, to be treated like a normal person.

The other thing she needed was help with all these files and records.

"You want me to have my brother killed because the paperwork isn't in order?" She set down the file she was holding and stretched her arms over her head. They'd been in here for hours. The first thirty minutes had consisted of Franco darting from cabinet to cabinet and box to box, commenting on the wealth of information. The second thirty minutes had been Franco getting increasingly irate as she pointed out the issues she was having finding and organizing the materials she'd brought out of storage in her quest to figure out why Franco's grandfather hadn't been called to the altar. When she got to the secret boxes in the Victrola, Franco had descended into wordless sounds of horror.

"Isn't he supposed to be punished for breaking the rules?"

"He *was* punished, that's why I'm the Grand Master."

"And what about this? How will he be punished for this?"

"His punishment is that he has to keep working on my father's journals."

"That's a drop in the bucket."

"Not knowing what's *in* that particular drop almost got him killed. I don't want to wind up in that same situation. I have no idea how many people there are like you—their families have drifted away, and they know pieces of information about us, but don't know enough to keep our secrets."

"You should have an archivist."

"I think one of my father's councilors acted as an archivist."

"A terrible one."

"Will you be one of my councilors?" she asked softly.

"Of course." Franco's immediate answer made her feel good, as if in him, she really had an ally with no ulterior allegiances.

Juliette released the tension she didn't realize she was carrying. The task she'd set for herself—to make sure she never faced a situation like the one her brother had, and to find everyone who might know about the Trinity Masters—was Herculean at best. Yet, she was terrified to ask for help. The Grand Masters gave orders, they didn't issue requests. "At least most of the current files are in good shape."

"Are they?" Franco held up a file and shook it. "Those are what I'm going through right now. Every file is completely different. Some are chronological with the birth certificate at the front, some start with the newest information. Some have copies of passports and driver's licenses; others have a sheet of paper with the information handwritten on it. Some have summary pages, others are just a mess of random information..."

Deciding arm stretches weren't enough, Juliette rose to her feet and did a full-body stretch, arching her back. When she realized Franco had stopped talking, she looked over. His gaze trailed over her, his eyes hot and heavy with desire.

Juliette's heartbeat quickened and she licked her lips. Maybe it was time to really make this office her own and have sex on the desk.

Then again, she can't have been the first Grand Master to have done that. Ew. Maybe she needed a new desk.

In the short time she'd spent being grossed out by the idea of having sex on the same desk where her parents might have, Franco had once again been distracted by the file in his hand.

"I mean, look at Devon's. His file is excellent. An itemized list of contents, a page on his trinity—oh, uh, look, there's your name. Moving on...look at this, a nice summary of who he is, why he's a member, and what his best traits are."

Devon. What the hell was she going to do about Devon? Had he meant what he said about loving her?

She was so lost in her thoughts she almost missed what Franco was reading from the file.

"'...cover identity as a lobbyist. He specializes in asset cultivation and information gathering on locations in Eastern Europe and North Africa rated as near-future potential threats.'"

"Wait, what did you say?" Juliette stepped over a few boxes and dropped down beside Franco.

"I was reading off his summary page."

Juliette snatched it from his hand.

Devon Asher (D.A.) is an agent of the US Central Intelligence Agency. He was recruited by CIA Deputy H.M., friend of D.A.'s father P.

D.A. maintains a cover identity as a lobbyist. He specializes in asset cultivation and information gathering on locations in Eastern Europe and North Africa rated as near-future potential threats. He is the Trinity Masters' primary point of contact with the CIA and will become CIA Director. A list of assets and major projects is included in the file.

D.A. nominally works for the lobbying firm Copper One. Copper One CEO is P.D. Additional information about his lobbyist position and Copper One job can be found in the file.

"No." Juliette laid the file on the floor. "No."

"Juliette? What's wrong?"

"He can't be."

"He? You mean Devon?" Franco rubbed her arms, speaking gently. "Did you not know he was a CIA agent?"

"No. I believed him when he said he was a lobbyist." She felt sick, physically sick.

"Maybe this is the thing he said he wanted to tell you."

"You think?" Juliette snarled the words.

Franco held up his hands. "Sorry, I'm just trying to help."

Juliette stood and paced, kicking things out of her way (and ignoring Franco's pained noises) as she walked. "Check the list."

"What list?"

"In the file. Check the list of assets."

"Okay." Franco's tone was deferential. Later she could be grateful that he hadn't stormed away when she lashed out.

"Found it. In this well-organized file—"

"Francisco!"

"Okay, okay. It says...wait, this is a list of places and names, not assets."

"The names are the assets. Most CIA agents don't go running around under false identities like in the movies—those are clandestine services people, and they're more for show at this point." Juliette's hot anger gave way to a weary chill and she knelt beside Franco, careful not to look at the list. "Assets are informants—people who give the CIA agent information. Good agents have lots of assets and can gather information from the safety of their offices."

"You know a lot about it."

"Because that's what I was supposed to be."

"You were supposed to be in the CIA?"

"Yes. I'm the perfect candidate—well educated, speak

multiple languages, familiar with different customs because I've traveled all my life. It's what my father wanted me to do. Up until the summer after I graduated high school, I thought he wanted me to be a lawyer. The file said Devon was recruited by H.M.? That's Harold Martin; he was the former CIA Deputy Director. He's a member and he tried to recruit Devon and me. I know because we talked about it.

"I'd just come back from a summer in Europe. I thought Mr. Martin was a lawyer, thought I was meeting with him to talk about my college plans. I'd already decided I wasn't going to be a lawyer and was going to focus on international-aid work.

"Both Devon and I said no. At least I thought we did. He *told* me he did."

"Why didn't you want to be a CIA agent?"

"The CIA is like the Trinity Masters—secretive, powerful, and they'll do whatever it takes to get what they want. Unlike the CIA, the Trinity Masters protects its people. Assets and agents of the CIA are in the line of fire, and if something goes wrong, they get no help."

Franco's brows were drawn together with concern and concentration. "You thought Devon said no when he was recruited."

"Yes. The same way Sebastian and I did."

"Sebastian?"

"My best friend. You'll meet him soon—assuming the jerk ever shows up."

"Sebastian Stewart?"

Juliette sucked in a breath. "Let me see that file."

Franco slapped it closed. "I don't think that's a good idea."

"Give it to me."

Franco took her hand. "I may not have grown up with Devon, but after last night I'd say I know him." Franco leered comically, but Juliette didn't laugh. His face sobered. "He loves you. No matter what it says in this file."

"Let me get it over with."

Franco flipped open to the page he'd found and handed it to her. The asset list was a printout of an email sent by Devon to Harold Martin under the guise of offering him a vacation.

Harold,

It was good to see you. Hope we can get together again soon. Here's the list of travel options Copper One would be happy to offer you. The first half of the list is places where we have active contracts. Let me know if you want any more information on any of them.

London
Rome
Rio
Istanbul
Ankara
Copenhagen
Edinburgh
Berlin
Sana
-

Paris
Cairo
Belmopan
San Jose

Handwritten to the right of each city was a person's name. It wasn't the most sophisticated code, but if only Devon and Harold knew the correlation between city and person, it was secure enough.

Her name was next to Paris.

"I'm sorry, Juliette."

"I never agreed to this. I never sent him any information. It means that these people," she pointed to the second half of the list, "aren't knowing assets, but somehow he's getting information from us."

"Are all these people members?"

"There are a few names I don't recognize, but most I do. And according to this, Sebastian is an active, knowing asset." Juliette's stomach rolled as she looked at the name next to London. "He turned down Mr. Martin, same as Devon and me. Sebastian and I both wanted to be aid workers. We took a stand, said that we wouldn't be part of a system that had caused so much damage in the past. But it looks like he was lying to me, too."

"Maybe there's a reason they didn't say anything."

"Sebastian is my best friend. He was the first person I told about becoming Grand Master. Devon was going to be my husband. What reason could be good enough?"

Franco took the file from her and set it down. "You're the kind of woman a man would do anything to impress." He ran one finger down her cheek. "The face that launched a thousand ships."

"And burned the towers of Ilium? I'm hardly Helen of Troy."

"You are, even if you don't mean to be."

"Lovely. I'm just another pretty prize for men to use as an excuse." Juliette pushed to her feet.

"That's not what I meant."

"But that's what I am—the princess whose marriage was more important than she was, the pretty blonde who drives men to do stupid things and becomes their excuse for bad behavior."

Pain and anger were coiling inside her, a hot, dark snake slithering through her torso. "I'm done. I'm done being anyone's prize."

"Okay."

Franco's mild reply took the wind out of her sails. "That's it? That's all you're going to say?"

"Yep. You're right—I shouldn't have tried to explain away their assholeness. I don't know what you're feeling, but I can empathize."

Juliette hopped up onto the edge of the desk. "Thank you."

"You're welcome."

They sat in silence, Juliette struggling to come to terms with what she'd just learned. "It wouldn't hurt so much if it weren't for last night."

"I'm not making excuses for him, but I know Devon loves you. He loves you, and he clearly knows you'd hate him if you knew what he did. It may not be right, but people do stupid things for love."

"No wonder Sebastian kept asking about the files. They must have realized that once I was Grand Master, I'd learn the truth."

"And you'd have the ability to have them killed."

Juliette laughed. "You're rather bloodthirsty."

"It's rare that I meet someone who actually has the ability to order a hit."

"I'm not a mob boss."

"But you could be." Franco's expression was almost envious.

"And here I thought you would be a voice of restraint."

Franco's head was bent over the next file. "Ha. You should have waited to put me on the small council."

"It's not the small council. This isn't *Game of Thrones* either."

"But it could be."

Juliette rolled her eyes. Her stomach was still in knots but Franco's silliness made her feel better. The urge to find both

Sebastian and Devon and scream at them was clawing and tingling under her skin.

She went around to take a seat at the desk, nearly tripping over her bag in the process. Pulling out a sheet of stationary, she dashed off a note to Devon and called the courier service. She then ran it upstairs, passing it off to a deliveryman who assumed he was there on library business. While she had cell service, she took the time to send Sebastian an angry text message.

When she returned to the headquarters, Franco had moved to the table and there seemed to be even more files out on the floor in piles. He'd found some hot-pink Post-Its (why did Harrison have hot-pink Post-Its?) and was creating some sort of labeling grid on the surface of the table.

Leaving him to it, she went back to the desk, almost tripping on her bag a second time.

Picking up the duffle, she pulled out the box Franco had brought her and put it on the desk, then added the files from home to the stack of current members. Franco kept a sharp eye on her, clearly feeling proprietary about the papers. Raising her hands in a sign of peace, she returned to the desk.

The box was a puzzle, the mystery a good distraction. While mentally composing precisely what she'd say to Devon, she broke the wax seal—which was just a dollop of wax, despite the fact that she knew the Grand Master had a wax stamp. She'd seen her father use it.

She opened the carved wooden box. It smelled of cedar and almonds, and the interior compartment was much smaller than she'd expected, the sides of the box each about an inch thick, which explained why it was so heavy.

Inside was a pen, paintbrush and a small glass vial. Each item was carefully held in place by small wood props built into the bottom of the box. The vial's cork has either rotted away or fallen out, because there was nothing left in the vial. She picked it up and carefully sniffed, jerking her head back. Whatever had been in there, it now smelled like a combination of lemon and rotting almonds.

Next she picked up the pen. It was heavy gold-toned metal shaped into a sharp-edged geometric pattern. As she turned it in her hand, the edges proved how sharp they were, cutting into her finger.

Yelping, she dropped the pen and stuck her finger in her mouth.

"You okay?" Franco looked up.

She took her finger from her mouth. "I opened the mystery box."

"What's in it?" Franco came over to look.

"A pen, a paintbrush and an empty vial."

"Huh." He studied the open box. "That's odd. Do these things have any significance to the Trinity Masters?"

"Not that I know of. There might be something in the records..."

"Is that a hint to get back to work?"

"Nice try pretending you aren't loving this."

"Love-hate. It's a love-hate kind of thing."

When Franco went back to the papers, Juliette returned to the box. The most puzzling thing was the paintbrush. She took everything out. Once again giving herself a paper-cut-like injury from the ridiculous pen.

Sucking on her injured finger, she used her free hand to poke around the inside of the box, and was rewarded for her efforts when her nail caught in a small divot. She pried the bottom panel up, uncovering a folded sheet of paper hidden inside.

"Eureka."

CHAPTER TWELVE

What a complete clusterfuck this day had turned out to be. He'd handled the issue with Sebastian, but now he had mountains of information to try to sort through and verify with other assets and surveillance.

And then the messenger had arrived, bearing a note from the Grand Master. This time it had clearly been Juliette's handwriting —she wasn't trying to disguise it. The note had been signed "G.M."

Respect for the Grand Master had been instilled into him since he was a baby, and as he walked down the marble hallway he had to remind himself that Juliette's word was now law.

There hadn't been instructions as to where he was to go, but since it had been a formal note, he stopped and put on a robe, forgoing taking off his other clothes. If at all possible, he'd rather not be naked and vulnerable for what was undoubtedly going to be a very crappy conversation.

Pulling the hood up, he went to the altar room, figuring that was the best place to wait.

And wait he did, for nearly two hours—until the sound of

panicked shouts had him running for one of the shadowed arches in the back wall.

This was absolutely terrifying. Franco sat back, staring at the pile he'd dubbed "mysteries". The Trinity Masters' files and records contained information that could change how the US saw its own history. There was at least a lifetime worth of work for someone like him in just this small stack of paper, let alone the boxes and mounds scattered on the floor.

"We're getting married, right? I mean, you and me?" He adjusted the piece of fabric he was using in lieu of gloves to handle the papers. "Because I need access to this."

"You want to get married so you can work on our archive?" Juliette's voice sounded a bit odd. She'd been muttering about lemon juice a few minutes ago, and even snuck upstairs, returning with a to-go cup of lemon wedges. He'd asked what she was doing but she waved him away.

"No, I want to get married because I'm falling in love with you and you're gorgeous, but now we *need* to get married. You need me to do this."

"You're one of my councilors. You're going to work on this even if we don't get married." She coughed.

"Before I realized it was you, I was going to ask the Grand Master if I could marry you and Devon."

Juliette wheezed. "Devon?"

He flipped the page. Was this a map? It looked like a map. He loved maps.

"Franco!" Her exclamation didn't have the force of a few minutes ago. She coughed again.

"What?"

"You seriously wanted to be in a trinity with Devon and me?"

"Of course. He loves you, you love him. The first time I saw you together I knew there was something between the two of you."

"Devon and I... Devon and I..."

Her voice trailed off, and the hairs on the back of Franco's neck stood on end. "Juliette?"

Her face was flushed and she was breathing hard.

Franco jumped out of his chair. "Juliette?"

"I don't...feel good."

He touched her forehead. "You're hot." He leaned her back in the desk chair, listening to her shallow breathing. "You were fine a couple hours ago."

Juliette opened her eyes, gaze darting across the ceiling. "Hard to. Breathe." She clawed at the desk, grabbing a sheet of paper and balling it up in her hand.

Franco grabbed his cell phone from his pocket. No reception. There was a phone on the desk. He picked it up, ready to call 911.

Call them and tell them what? That he was in the underground headquarters of a secret society? He needed to get her upstairs to the library.

Picking her up in his arms, Franco ran out of the Grand Master's office—and had no idea which hallway to take. There were three options and he didn't remember which way they'd come in.

Heart hammering in his chest, Franco picked the right-hand option and started jogging, yelling as he went. "Help! Can anyone hear me? Help!"

She said they'd be the only people in here, and yelling was probably futile. Whatever was wrong with Juliette had happened fast, and that was never a good sign. By the time he figured out how to get the hell out of here, it might be too late.

He was hoping for a miracle.

"Franco? Juliette!"

Devon nearly ran into Franco as he entered the dark hallway beyond the arch. Juliette was limp in his arms, her face flushed and breath reedy.

"Help me get her out of here."

Devon didn't ask any questions. Now wasn't the time. Handle the crisis at hand then investigate.

He resisted the urge to snatch Juliette from the other man's arms. If it had been anyone else he would have, but, unexpectedly, he trusted Franco. Maybe it was the grim look of determination on his face. Maybe it was the undeniable connection he'd felt to Franco last night.

"Have you called 911?" Devon smashed the button for the elevator.

"No. I wasn't sure what to do. She has a phone in her office." Franco shifted his hold of Juliette enough to shed the robe. When Devon reached to take her, he leaned away, keeping her in his arms.

"Her office?"

Franco leapt into the elevator the instant the door opened. "The Grand Master's office. I assume you know."

"I know. *You* know?"

"Yes. I'm going to sit on the small council, too."

"The what?" Devon had his phone out, 911 dialed. The second the door opened and they were above ground, he was going to hit send. "Wait. You're going to be one of her councilors?"

"Don't worry, I told her the three of us should get married."

What?

He didn't have time to deal with any of what Franco had just said. The doors opened. Devon hit send.

"911, what's your emergency?"

"My wife collapsed and is having trouble breathing. We're at the Boston Public Library."

"Hang up," Juliette whispered.

Devon ended the call without hesitation, ignoring Franco's protest. "What's going on, Jules?"

"Poison." Her eyes were closed, but she raised one hand, showing him the cuts on her fingers. The other hand was clenched around a sheet of paper.

Devon's vision dimmed and his stomach rolled. He couldn't lose her.

"Poison? What?" Franco headed for the door. "Call 911 back."

Devon grabbed him, pushing him toward a table. "Set her down."

There must have been something in his voice, something that let the other man know that he would not hesitate to kill if needed. Franco laid her on the table.

Devon leaned down so she wouldn't have to speak above a whisper. "What else do I need to know?"

"Almonds." In the light of the rare-book room, her skin was flushed as if she had a sunburn, her lips turning blue. Her breathing was ragged.

"I understand." Devon wanted to hold her, kiss her, tell her it would all be okay. He did none of that.

She seemed to relax, as if she trusted him to take care of her. Praying that was true, and praying he could save her, Devon dialed his phone.

"Hello, Alexis? This is Devon Asher. I need your help. Do you have a cyanide-poisoning kit?"

"She knows."

Devon ignored Franco and dropped into a chair in Michael's office at Boston General Hospital. He wasn't even sure what time it was anymore and he was exhausted. Franco was stripped down to his underwear, a blanket over his shoulders. They'd both handed over their clothes and showered as a precaution, in case there were trace amounts of the poison on them. Devon had borrowed a pair of scrubs and run back to his hotel then headed out to investigate. He hated being away from Juliette when she was ill, but he knew her well enough to know she'd want action, not useless waiting.

"Why didn't you tell her the truth?"

"Shut up." The words were too quiet for Franco to hear.

"I saw her face. She was heartbroken."

"I said shut up."

"No."

Devon was too tired to stop himself. He exploded out of the chair, pinning Franco against the wall with his forearm across his throat.

"You have no right to question me. I've done my duty. My whole life I've done my duty. Juliette got to take a stand, to be idealistic. I didn't."

Franco was eerily calm, not resisting him in any way. Devon eased back. Franco grabbed his shoulder and flipped their positions, pinning *Devon* against the wall, the calm demeanor a ruse.

"If you loved her, you wouldn't have used her."

"Used her?" Devon closed his eyes. "What exactly does she know?"

"She knows you're a CIA agent and that you've been using her for information without her knowledge."

"Fuck." This was worse than he'd imagined. Everything was spiraling out of control. "I hoped...I hoped she'd only figured out I was CIA."

"If our marriage is going to work, you're going to have to tell the truth."

Devon opened one eye. "Our marriage?"

"I told her that the three of us should get married."

Devon eased himself away from the wall, forcing Franco back a step. "I know how Juliette feels about the CIA and what I do. She made it very clear years ago. After last night, there might have been a way for us to reconcile, but now..." He swallowed, forcing his voice to remain level though it wanted to break from pain. "I'm sure you'll be part of the trinity she eventually assigns herself, but I won't be."

"She loves you—she's loved you for a long time."

"According to her, it's not love, it's brainwashing."

"Juliette doesn't seem like the kind of person who can be brainwashed."

That startled a laugh out of Devon. "No. She's not."

"I think that's what makes her angry, what frightens her. She's tried to talk herself out of loving you, and she can't."

"Franco...don't. Please."

"Don't what?"

"Don't give me hope."

The door opened and Alexis stepped in. Her face was grim. As one, they turned to her.

"You were right, Devon. It's cyanide poisoning."

"Fuck," Franco whispered.

"Will she be okay?"

"Yes. It wasn't a huge dose and we got to her in time for the hydroxocobalamin to be effective."

Both men sighed in relief. Juliette would be okay. Devon hadn't taken a true deep breath since she'd whispered "almonds", prompting him to inhale and realize she smelled like bitter almonds, the telltale sign of cyanide poison.

"How?" Devon needed answers.

"I'm not sure. I've only seen this kind of thing when it's been inhaled. Usually cyanide poisoning is accidental and happens when there's been a fire, particularly in a place with a lot of plastic. But you," she gestured to Franco, "said you were with her. If you aren't feeling sick, then it wasn't inhaled, meaning it was either ingested or injected."

"I brought something for you to test." Devon took a bag from his pocket and held it out. In it was a gold pen he'd found on Juliette's desk. "Be careful, it's sharp, and it looks like there's blood on it."

Alexis held up the bag to examine the pen. "A poisoned pen? If it were coated in cyanide and she cut herself on it, that might be enough to transmit it."

"I saw her sucking on her finger after she cut it, but that can't be it." Franco shook his head. "The pen was in the box I gave her."

Devon bowed his head, giving himself a moment of respite. He reached into his coat. "That's what I was afraid of." He pulled out his gun and pointed it at Franco.

"Whoa! What the fuck?" Franco raised his hands in the universal "don't shoot" posture. The blanket fell to the ground.

"Devon, is this necessary?" Alexis looked weary.

"Yes." Devon held his phone in his other hand, ready to call for a cleanup crew. "His grandfather was a member, but never called to the altar. I'm thinking there was a reason for that."

"Are you going to shoot me? Actually shoot me?"

"The fact that you're asking makes me think you haven't been paying attention. I will do *anything* to protect her."

"You mean protect the Trinity Masters."

Devon lowered his voice so only the two of them could hear. "Juliette *is* the Trinity Masters."

"Devon. Stop." Juliette's voice was weak, but they reacted as if she'd yelled the command.

Devon's whole body started to shake with relief when he saw her standing in the doorway. She seemed tiny in the too-large hospital gown that hung from her shoulders. Her skin was no longer flushed, her lips their normal color. If anything, she was pale, the dark circles under her eyes standing out.

"Juliette."

Their gazes met. He expected to see anger. Expected her to rage and throw things. He'd lied to her. He'd had Sebastian help him get her email passwords so he could use the information she gathered for her humanitarian work to inform the CIA's activities in the regions where she'd been. He'd been hoping to someday come clean and somehow make it okay once they were married.

Once she couldn't get away.

He was such an ass.

"I'm sorry." The words were heavy, conveying years of regret and missteps.

Juliette nodded. The anger he'd expected to see wasn't there. "I know." She seemed calm and in control. She seemed like the Grand Master.

Juliette turned to Franco. "Did you know?"

"Can you make him put down the gun?"

"Did you know?" Juliette's tone didn't change. She was like a stone—not necessarily unfeeling, but hard and immovable.

Franco seemed to sense the change. He lowered his hands a fraction as his gaze searched her face. "Did I know what?"

"Did you know about the poison?"

"No."

"Alexis, please test the pen."

"Of course. It will only take a second."

When she left the room, the three of them stood in silence. Tension ebbed and flowed between them as if it were a living thing.

"Lower the gun, but don't put it away."

Devon dropped his arm to his side.

Franco lowered his hands. "Juliette, I didn't know."

"Either you truly *didn't* know, or you're a very skilled assassin."

"Assassin? You don't really think...I didn't even know you existed until two weeks ago!"

"The Grand Master always risks assassination. Our secrets are kept but not absolute." Devon spoke to Franco but he was looking at Juliette. "I spoke to Harrison and he told me about the attempt on his life. There are some who might not accept Juliette as the new Grand Master. They won't know who she is, but there's no hiding that she's a woman."

"Which is why no one can know about the poison. I can't appear weak. That means it's up to the three of us to solve this mystery."

"Could it have been accidental?" Franco sounded hopeful.

"No. You heard Alexis. Burning plastic is what causes accidental poisoning."

"Shit. I swear I didn't know. I never opened the box."

Juliette took a step and wobbled. Both Franco and Devon lunged to help her but she waved them back and took a seat. "And your grandfather never opened the box?"

"No."

"I think he was meant to. I think the poison was meant for Franco's grandfather."

"Why?"

"Because of this." Juliette held out a crumpled sheet of paper. "My father used to tell me stories about how his own father, my grandfather, would send messages using invisible ink, ink that had to be brushed with lemon juice to make it appear. There was a vial and a paintbrush in the box. I think at one point the vial held lemon juice, and the paintbrush was used to apply it."

Franco yelped in excitement and started moving toward

Juliette. Devon raised the gun and cleared his throat. Franco froze then bared his teeth in a snarl of frustration.

Juliette's lips twitched as she tried to hide a smile. That little hint of a smile allowed much of the tension to drain out of Devon's shoulders. He kept the gun pointed on Franco, but was really hoping he wouldn't have to shoot the other man.

"This sheet was hidden under the false bottom of the box. It just a bunch of random words in Spanish, but when you apply lemon juice there's a message."

"What does it say?" Devon asked.

"It says something along the lines of 'decode this and bring the answers to Boston'."

"Meaning my grandfather was supposed to find and read the letter."

"Yes."

Franco shook his head. "Then why wouldn't he have opened the box?"

"And why would there be a poisoned pen inside?" Devon asked.

"That's what we're going to figure out." Juliette stood. "The gala is in two days."

"We should wait until you're better." Devon didn't like the idea of her facing down the assembled Trinity Masters while still recovering.

"We can't wait. You know that."

"Can I have the letter?" Franco looked at Devon—more specifically, at the gun.

Juliette nodded and Devon lowered the gun as Alexis returned.

"The pen tested positive. I know you're going to want it back to study it, but it's too dangerous." Alexis looked grim. "I'll handle disposal. Devon, Franco, if you feel any shortness of breath, you need to head immediately to the emergency room."

"Thank you, Alexis," Devon said.

"That cyanide was weak—if it had been full strength you could have been in serious trouble. Most likely the reason you got sick is because you sucked on your finger when you cut it. Do you want me to call Harrison?" Alexis picked up Juliette's wrist as she spoke, checking her pulse.

"No. I can handle this."

Alexis nodded, but she looked worried. "You have to rest. You might feel okay right now, but that's probably adrenaline. I have a private room set up for you. When you're done here, come to my office and I'll take you to a room where no one will bother you."

"I'm going to go home."

"No, you're not. You're at least going to spend the night in the hospital. You were poisoned."

Juliette looked poised to protest then seemed to deflate. "Okay. Thanks, Alexis."

Once Alexis left, Juliette gave Franco the letter before she, too, turned to leave.

"Juliette, wait."

She paused, turned back to him, and Devon got a horrible sense of *deja vu*.

"I need time, Devon. Just need time."

Then she was gone, leaving Devon standing with a gun dangling from his hand, Franco frowning down at the crumpled paper.

Franco looked up. "What are we going to do?"

"We? I just held a gun on you."

"I'm surprised you didn't shoot me."

"Usually I'm a fan of ask-questions-later, except when it comes to shooting people."

"Hard to torture information out of someone when they're dead."

"True."

"That was supposed to be a joke."

Devon shrugged, but he was biting back a smile.

"Fucking CIA." Franco frowned at the letter. "I need lemons. Where would I find lemons?"

"Come on. I'll help you."

"Can I have some pants first?"

Devon laughed. He couldn't help himself. Everything about his life was serious and dramatic. Someone like Franco, who could take even the direst situation and add a note of sometimes unintentional comedy, was wonderful.

"First pants. Then lemons."

THE REALITY of it didn't hit her until late that night. Juliette jerked awake, clawing at her throat, the memory of the poison-induced strangulation enough to have her crying out.

Arms came around her, comforting and cradling her.

"Devon?"

"I'm here, Jules."

"Franco?"

"Shh, you're safe, *querida*."

The hospital bed wasn't big enough for them to join her, but they held her hands, stroked her arms. Protected on either side, Juliette fell back to sleep.

CHAPTER THIRTEEN

It was too risky for Juliette to go back to the house on Winthrop Square, since the other legacies were arriving in advance of the gala. Devon upgraded his room to a suite and took her to his hotel once Alexis okayed her to leave the hospital on Friday afternoon. Devon made sure she was comfortable and left once she was happily chowing down on room service. By the time he came back, she was once more asleep.

Franco showed up, suitcase in hand, a few hours later. He was taking the other bedroom in the suite. They spent the day working, sometimes together, sometimes separately. Progress was frustratingly slow, but Devon was glad he wasn't trying to do this alone. Franco had taken on the task of checking through the mountains of paperwork in the Grand Master's office for clues. He hadn't come up with anything, at least not yet, but they were eliminating possibilities. As the day went on, Devon was increasingly sure that this hadn't been a circuitous attempt on Juliette's life.

He was glad he had something to do. She'd been sick, but it

rattled him that Juliette hadn't exploded in anger when she saw him. He was dreading the conversation they were going to have when she woke up.

Near midnight, Franco rose and stretched. "I'm tired. Let's go to bed. Tomorrow I'm going to call my father. Maybe he'll remember something about the box."

"Fair enough." Devon rubbed the back of his neck and closed his laptop.

Franco headed to the bedroom. The wrong bedroom.

"Other way," Devon said.

"Isn't Juliette in this room?"

"Yes."

"Then this is where I'm going."

"I was going to stay with her tonight."

"We'll both stay with her."

Devon considered the other man. "Good idea."

THE MATTRESS SANK under their weight, one man on each side of her. The covers were pushed aside, and for a moment she shivered as the cool air touched her bare skin. Then their hands were on her naked flesh, warm palms and firm fingers kneading and stroking.

They eased her hands away from her throat, kissed and stroked her shoulders and cheeks. The poison still lingered in her blood, making her body ache as if she were recovering from the flu. They treated her as if she was made of glass, taking their time.

Devon slid down the bed, easing her legs apart. "Tell me if you're too tired for this."

"No, not too tired."

"Let me hold you." Franco slid in place against the headboard, her back resting on his chest.

She could feel his hard cock against the small of her back.

They kissed and stroked, comforting her without words. Devon lowered his head between her legs, kissing her pussy as Franco toyed with her nipples.

She came once, and then Devon moved away, Franco taking his place.

"Spread her open with your fingers. She likes it when you fuck her with your tongue. Rub your nose on her clit while you do it."

Devon coached Franco on how to touch her, how to pleasure her. When the sensation became too intense, coming so soon after her first orgasm, Devon held her down, his hands gentle but strong restraints, his kiss muffling her gasps of pleasure.

She came a second time, her sweaty body sinking bonelessly into the mattress. Franco slid between her legs, his cock rubbing between the lips of her sex.

"Kiss him, keep him calm." Devon had climbed off the bed.

Juliette stroked Franco's face. "Hi," she whispered.

He kissed her cheek. "Hi," he replied.

The mattress dipped under Devon's weight. He held a tube of lube.

Juliette turned wide eyes on Franco. "Are you okay with this?"

"Yes. I want to be with you, both of you, in every way." Franco smiled.

"Have you ever had anal sex before?" Juliette asked.

"With a dude? No."

"What?"

"I had this one girlfriend, in college... It's a long story."

"I can be in the middle," she offered.

"No, you need to rest." Devon wrapped an arm around Franco's chest, pulling the other man up. Franco turned his head and they kissed. The sight of Devon's muscled arm across Franco's equally muscled chest was delightfully arousing.

When Franco once more hovered over her, propped on his elbows, his legs spread, forcing hers even wider apart, Devon opened the tube, the click of the cap loud.

Franco tensed and Juliette set to work calming him. She stroked his head and shoulders. Kissed him gently. She knew the moment Devon penetrated him with a finger because he tensed, then shivered. Devon was a skilled lover. He'd introduced Juliette to anal sex also.

"Are you ready, Franco?"

"Yes."

Devon slid into place, kneeling behind Franco, his hands on the other man's hips. Franco's jaw clenched.

Juliette ran her hands down Franco's sides until they lay beside Devon's.

"I want to feel you both."

Devon met her gaze as he pressed into Franco, who groaned at the penetration. He was stiff for a few minutes, but Devon's patience and Juliette's attention soon eased the tension from his muscles.

Then Devon began to thrust in earnest, his cock pushing Franco's hips forward so that Juliette was penetrated, too. Franco came first, the combined sensations of Juliette's pussy around his cock and Devon's dick in his ass, stimulating his prostate, causing him to shake from the force of his orgasm.

When he collapsed and rolled away Devon pulled off the condom he was wearing, tossing it aside. He sank into Juliette, who wrapped her legs around his waist, coming as he thrust in the first time.

She tingled with residual pleasure as he thrust his way to

orgasm. Then they curled around each other, content and quiet.

"I could have lost you."

Juliette frowned as she woke up, struggling to shift from pleasant dream to the tension-filled darkness, *deja vu* adding to the sense of unreality. She lifted her head off Devon's chest. Though he'd whispered, she'd felt the rumble of his words.

"Devon?"

"You could have died. I could have lost you." He sounded raw, his voice like rocks cracking together.

"But I didn't die." Her heart couldn't stand to hear the pain in his tone. She brushed her fingers over his chest and shoulders. "You saved me. You understood."

"Jules, I've been an ass to you. I know that. I just...I figured once we were married..." His tone had changed to sheepish.

Juliette lifted her hands off his bare skin. "I couldn't get away?"

He rubbed his face, the movement barely visible in the ambient light that filtered in through the window.

Now fully awake, Juliette sat up. Franco, who'd been asleep at her back, did the same. "Do you two always have dramatic conversations in the middle of the night?"

Juliette ignored him. "It's not like I could have changed my mind and called off the engagement. Why didn't you tell me the truth?"

"I see you a couple times a year, and when I do see you, half the time you're busy making it clear that you hate me. When was I supposed to start the conversation that would guarantee you never spoke to me again?"

"It's my fault?" Juliette's hands curled into fists.

"That's not what I'm saying."

Franco grabbed a sheet off the floor and tucked it around Juliette. "You have to give him a chance to explain."

The speeches she'd prepared when she wrote the summons were forgotten. Franco was calm and resolute, his hands on her shoulders urging her to stay, to listen. Tension radiated off Devon. When Juliette took a deep breath and let it out, loudly enough that they both could hear, Devon seemed to relax.

He cleared his throat. "By the time you decided you wanted nothing to do with the agency, I'd already been working for them for a long time.

"I started out as an asset when I was eighteen. I officially joined the agency midway through college. I was recruited the same way you were, just five years earlier."

"So you've been lying to me for years." The words were bitter, and only Franco's hand kept her on the bed.

"No. I've been hiding the truth from you for years. I thought you'd change your mind and it wouldn't matter. When I realized you wouldn't, I didn't know how to tell you. I always assumed we'd end up in the agency together."

"Information. What information were you getting from me?"

He sighed and pressed the heels of his hands against his eyes. "I ghosted your computer and email accounts."

"You son of a bitch."

"Damn it, Juliette. You know how this works. I don't want to torture information out of locals, or put guns into the hands of people who aren't trained to use them."

"Then what do you do?" Franco's question was genuinely curious, and as was becoming custom, his apparent failure to react to the tension between Juliette and Devon helped ease the situation. His avid, almost lewd curiosity let the air out of Juliette's balloon of outrage.

Devon's snort-laugh was weary. "The best information comes from either locals or aid workers. People like Juliette." He sat up. "The best way to stop terrorism is to eliminate environments where terrorism thrives. Water, food, doctors—these are all things we can provide, if we know they're needed."

"All those times other charities stepped in?" Her work with North Star had overlapped with the arrival of other charities or initiatives multiple times.

"Not every time, but when you had intel on high-risk areas, I did my best to make sure the region got whatever you said it needed."

"And what about the rest of my email?"

"I never read it."

Juliette snorted. "Right."

"I'm serious. Do you think I wanted to read about the people you were dating and sleeping with? That would have killed me."

"I'm supposed to believe that you—"

"Yes," Franco said.

"Excuse me?" Juliette twisted to peer at him in the darkness.

"Yes, you're supposed to believe him."

"Stay out of this," she demanded.

"No. If we're going to be in this together, I'm not going to stay out of it. Your past impacts me."

"You have no say in whether or not we end up together." Juliette kept the words cold.

"I know that, but I can't imagine *not* spending the rest of my life with the two of you." Franco spoke simply, the absolute truth of what he was saying clear in his voice.

Once again, his words sapped the tension from the room.

"Neither can I." Devon reached out and laid his hand over Franco's on Juliette's shoulder. "My future has always had you in it, Jules. Always. I love Rose, too, but not the way I love you." He squeezed, emphasizing their physical connection. "Or the way I'm coming to love Franco."

Could she forgive Devon?

Would she have done any differently if she were in his position?

It was time to grow up.

"I want to be angry with you, both of you. Devon, for lying to me for years. Franco, for assuming things I may not be ready to commit to."

Both men stiffened, the air around their little trio tightening as they waited for the "but".

"But, I need you both. I was never meant to be Grand Master, and it's going to be hard." Franco scooted closer to her until he supported her back. Devon picked up her hands and kissed them. "I'm a woman, I'm young, and I don't even like half of our rules. I need both of you to help me do this."

"Anything you need, *querida*."

"Always. My heart is yours."

"Devon, I've already asked Franco, but now I'm asking you. Will you be one of my councilors?"

"Yes. I'm honored." He kissed her hands again.

Without discussing it, they all shifted, with Devon propped against the headboard, Franco sprawled out near the foot of the bed. Juliette lay back against Devon. He was solid and warm—familiar in a way that felt like home. Franco tugged on her legs until they were draped over his hip then massaged her feet with one hand. They lay in companionable silence.

"Can I be the master of ships?" Franco's voice was hopeful.

"What?" Devon's voice was husky with sleep.

Juliette sighed. "It's not the small council from *Game of Thrones*."

"*Song of Ice and Fire*," Devon corrected.

There was a pregnant silence.

"You read high fantasy?" Juliette asked. How many other things didn't she know about Devon?

"Closeted geek." Franco yawned and stretched. "I can see it. I bet you're into cosplay, too."

"I am not."

"You'd make a good Jaime Lannister."

"Screw you."

"You did."

Devon mock growled. "I've changed my mind. I don't want him in the trinity."

"You know we need him." Juliette smiled. This was fun. When she'd imagined being married to Rose and Devon, nights spent lounging in bed and teasing one another had never seemed like a possibility. Intense, hardcore sex, sure. Teasing? Nope.

"You definitely need me. The two of you take yourselves way too seriously."

"Hey." Juliette jabbed him with her foot. "Okay, fine, you're right. We're no good as a couple."

"Couple? Couples are for amateurs." Devon tightened his arm around her, settling in as if he were going to sleep.

Silence surrounded them, warm and comfortable. As much as she wanted to stay here, live in this moment, Juliette couldn't ignore the future.

"The gala is tonight," she whispered.

"I hate to tell you this, but they're going to know you're a woman." Franco patted her calf.

"My fake deep voice wasn't convincing?"

"It was for a second, because I expected it to be a man."

"That's some misogyny right there," Devon said.

"Oh, like you wouldn't have assumed it was a guy." Franco sounded grumpy.

"Of course not."

"Correct me if I'm wrong, but until a couple of weeks ago, weren't you going to have two wives? *That's* some misogyny."

"Boys." They both shut up. Franco brought out Devon's fun side, which was nice to see, but there was a time and place, and now was not it. They had serious business to attend to. "I'm not going to try to disguise my voice. You're right, Franco. It wasn't convincing."

"Are you ready to face them all?" Devon asked.

"No." She laid her head back on Devon's shoulder and stared into the darkness. In that moment, the weight of her roles as Grand Master weighed heavy on her shoulders. "I'd planned to make some changes." Devon laced his fingers with hers and squeezed. Franco rubbed her foot. Their presence didn't lighten the load, but it made it more bearable. "I'd planned to abolish the arranged-marriage rule."

Devon went statue still at her back then hesitantly replied, "I don't want to fight with you, but—"

Juliette reached up and stopped Devon's words with her fingers. "I know. It was stupid of me to even consider changing our rules because I was upset. I don't want to make any other stupid mistakes."

"I know you said that this gala is important, but we need to figure out the whole poison thing, too," Franco said. "That's assuming Devon doesn't decide it was *me* trying to poison the Grand Master and shoot me."

"Just let me know. I'll shoot him."

Juliette ignored them with the grace of a queen. "More than just the poisoning. We still don't know why your grandfather was never called to the altar."

"So what do you need us to do, Grand Master?" There was no mocking in Devon's tone. He would wait for her orders, and Franco would follow his lead.

Juliette sat up. Dawn light was starting to show around the edge of the curtains. "First, coffee. Then let's make a plan."

"I'm making the coffee." Franco jumped off the bed. "You people have no idea how to make coffee."

"You people?" Juliette rose and opened the drapes.

"New Englanders. White people. Take your pick."

"I'll pretend that wasn't offensive." She raised her arms, stretching in the first rays of dawn.

"Juliette."

She turned when Devon said her name. He held out a hand. When she placed her fingers in his, he relaxed, a small smile curving the corners of his mouth.

"Master of Coin. I changed my mind, I want to be the Master of Coin."

Devon picked up a pillow and threw it at Franco. "Shut up. We're having a moment."

Franco rolled his eyes and pulled on his shirt. "You two are so dramatic. It's like you were raised in a secret cult or something...oh, wait."

"We're not a cult."

"Whatever you say." Franco dodged a second pillow and slapped Juliette's butt on his way out the door.

There was an awkward silence when it was just the two of them, reinforcing the need for Franco in their trinity.

"I'm sorry, Juliette."

"I'm sorry, too." She pulled on stretchy pants and a sweater. When she sat on the bed to put on socks, Devon took them from her. He knelt at her feet like a knight pledging fealty.

"Whatever you decide to do, whatever you need, I'll support you." He kissed each foot before putting the socks on.

"Thank you. I'll need it. I have an idea, a way to solve multiple problems at once, but I don't know how everyone else will react."

"Change is hard."

Juliette wiggled her toes in her socks then jumped to her feet.

"Well, change is coming. There's a new sheriff in town."

Devon groaned and started getting dressed. "He's rubbing off on you."

Juliette laughed, slapped Devon's butt and headed downstairs, ready to have her first council meeting. Members of the Trinity Masters may be powerful, dangerous people, but she was the Grand Master.

And she was about to change everything.

CHAPTER FOURTEEN

"Papa."

"Francisco. How are you?"

"I'm good."

"Marcia says you are not home, not at the foundation."

Franco reminded himself to tell Marcia to stop reporting on him to his parents. Though he was technically the foundation president, Marcia knew where the real power still lay—Franco's father. But it was his mother who liked to keep tabs on him.

"Tell Mama to stop making Marcia spy on me."

"She worries."

"Where are you right now?"

"Morocco. Did you see the video your mother posted to our YouTube channel?"

"No." Franco stifled a groan. His mother was a bit tech-mad. She'd started a Twitter account and YouTube channel to document their retirement travels. "I'll check it out after this."

"You better, before you talk to her again."

"I actually called because I have a question."

"Of course. Ask."

"It's about something of Grandfather's. It's that old box, the one he said belonged to the secret society."

"Oh, your grandfather and his stories. Why do you ask?"

"I'm doing some research on a photo I found. You'll love it. I'll show you when you get home. Anyway, while I was working on that, I looked at the box again. I'm thinking about opening it. Do you know why Grandfather never did?"

"He said that the person who delivered it to him warned him it was a test. If he didn't open the box, it would prove he could resist the temptation. He always said he was smarter than Pandora—he knew when to leave a box alone."

That didn't make any sense. The letter hidden inside the box had explicit instructions that Luis was to try to decode the list and then bring the answers to Boston. There was no way he could do that if he never found the letter.

"Do you remember anything else about it? Maybe about the man who gave him the box?"

"Now that I think of it…it wasn't a *man*. It was a woman. A beautiful red-haired woman, of course." Henry laughed. "His stories never had anything but beautiful women."

"That helps, thanks, Papa."

Franco hung up and relayed what he'd learned to Devon.

"He said that a beautiful red-haired woman delivered the box."

"My turn." Devon picked up his phone and placed a call to *his* father. Ewan was one of two, and of his two fathers, he'd always been closer to Ewan, though based on looks, Ted was probably his biological father. His career in the Navy meant Ted wasn't around much, but both men were good parents.

But Ewan had been a councilor to Juliette's father.

"Dad, it's me."

"Devon, how are you?"

"Busy. I have some things going on."

"Do you want me to call you back on the other line?" There was a secure landline in his parents' house that couldn't be traced or tapped.

"Not now. Hasn't reached that point yet. But I do need information."

"What kind?"

"Red-haired woman who delivered messages and packages in the late nineteen forties."

"Nineteen forties? Hmm."

Devon knew better than to interrupt while his dad was thinking. He glanced at his watch. The gala was in a matter of hours. He wanted to have answers before he walked into that room. If the threat was an old one, directed at someone besides Juliette, then there was no imminent danger. If the poison was meant for her, which seemed farfetched but not impossible, they would need to take extra precautions tonight.

"It might be Jessica Breton. She was a very visible member of your grandfather's generation."

"Would she have had any connection to the GM?"

"I don't know who her two, uh, friends were. I don't think anyone knew."

"Could it have *been* the GM?"

"No, but either she or one of her friends might have been councilors."

"That helps. Thanks, Dad."

"If you're in Boston for the party, be sure to say high to the Hancocks for me."

"I will. I'll call you afterwards." Devon put enough emphasis on the words to convey that there would be something worth talking about.

"Oh? I look forward to it."

He hung up.

"Were you speaking in code?" Franco asked.

"Old habits die hard. Jessica Breton."

"We're going to have to go to the office to check the files."

They were gathering up their things when Devon's phone rang. The display read "Parents-Private". Someone was calling him from the secure line.

"Dad?" he answered.

"No, it's Mom."

"Hi, Mom. Everything okay?"

"Your father told me you called. You were asking about Jessica Breton."

"Yes, do you know who her trinity was?"

"No, but be careful."

Devon sank to the edge of the bed. "Why?"

"There were rumors about Jessica. I remember hearing your grandmas talking about it." Devon's mother was a legacy also, her maiden name Butler.

"What were the rumors?"

"That she was a purist."

"A what?"

"A purist. In the early part of the war, there were rumors that some members were Nazi sympathizers. They were upset by the integration and social-justice initiatives the trinities were focused on."

"What do you mean?"

"In the nineteen thirties, a lot of members were recruited to help address issues around poverty, education and workers' rights. There were rumors that some legacy members weren't okay with that. They didn't like the focus, didn't like that these new members weren't from wealthy white backgrounds."

"And they were called purists?"

"Yes. But it was just rumors. I don't know how much that's worth."

"You might have just solved the mystery. Thanks, Mom."

When Devon hung up, Franco looked at him expectantly. "What was that?"

"My mother says the delivery woman may have been part of a racist subset of members who were active in the thirties and forties."

"The kind of people who wouldn't want my grandfather in their white-only club."

"Exactly."

"So Jessica sabotaged my grandfather by lying to him when she gave him the box. She told him not to open it when he was supposed to do the exact opposite."

"I think so." Devon shook his head in disgust.

"Then why the poison?"

"Backup plan? In case he did open it?"

"That makes sense. And when Grandfather never turned up with the answer, the Grand Master just forgot about him."

"No one should be forgotten." Devon checked his watch and cursed. "Juliette found poison meant for your family, to keep them from continuing as members. That answers one mystery, but raises more questions." Devon grabbed the garment bags off the bed.

"What questions?"

Devon pushed Franco out the door. They couldn't be late. Not tonight. "If these purists were close enough to the Grand Master to be trusted as messengers, how many other people did they either sabotage or outright kill?"

"I'll add it to the list of mysteries."

Devon laughed, pulling Franco against him and kissing his cheek. "You're so weird."

"Aw, you know you love it, Dev."

"Don't call me Dev."

"Why not, Dev?"

They were still bickering by the time they picked up Juliette, who'd gone to get ready at the townhouse. She laughed at their antics all the way to the library. When they parked, the amusement left her face.

The solemn trio made their way to the headquarters. It was time.

THE WHISPERS STARTED the moment she entered. The altar room and large foyer hallway were filled with people. Some wore the concealing gray robes of the Trinity Masters while others were in tuxedos and evening dresses. The Winter Gala always coincided with the library's black-tie fundraiser. Members would mingle at the fundraiser before slipping away and taking the hidden elevator to the real party.

Though there were hundreds of members, only a hundred or so attended these gatherings. Usually each trinity was able to send at least one person, and those who hadn't been called to the altar—the younger members—often came to revel in the still-novel aspects of the secret meetings.

There were no caterers, but silver tubs of ice held bottles of Champagne that was sipped out of realistic-looking plastic flutes.

Juliette wore the black robe and gold chain of the Grant Master. It rendered her anonymous, but she was shorter and slighter than her brother. The height difference was emphasized by the two men who walked behind and slightly to each side of her. Franco wore a gray robe with the hood down. Devon wore a tuxedo. He nodded to members he knew as they passed.

A ripple went through the room as people realized that the person in the Grand Master's robe was new. Plus, Devon's presence at the Grand Master's side wouldn't go unnoticed.

Though the identity of the Grand Master's council was secret, at events like this, it was fairly obvious who was close to the Grand Master, especially if that person chose not to go robed. Price Bennett, one of Harrison's former advisors, was well-known among the members, and it had always been clear that he was one of the councilors.

Yet he stood off to the side with his spouses, Deni and Gunner.

Franco rang the gong in the altar room, the reverberating sound heavy and solemn.

Juliette took her place behind the altar. Franco and Devon flanked her. Harrison, Alexis and Michael stood near the front of the crowd, Harrison's expression was worried. He whispered to Michael and Gunner, who melted back through the crowd, taking up positions in different places and carefully watching the reactions of those around them.

Price stepped forward, standing in front of the altar. They'd decided he was the best person to start the presentation, since he was well known. His support would carry weight.

Price waited until the crowd fell silent, those who were out in the hall crowding into the altar room. When all eyes were on him, he spoke. "Tonight we welcome a new Grand Master, even as we honor the service of the previous master, who can no longer shoulder the responsibility."

Unease rippled through the crowd, spreading out from Price as if he were the point where a stone had dropped into water. He stepped aside, revealing the cloaked figure of the Grand Master.

"I greet you at the dawn of a new day." Juliette projected so her voice carried, but had to pause as whispers and small sounds of surprise moved through the assemblage. Her voice was clearly feminine, her words unexpected.

"We are stronger than ever before, our dedication to our society second only to our commitment to our country."

There was a smattering of clapping and even some cheers from the oh-so-slightly drunk younger members.

"But our line is not unbroken, the story of our past is not complete."

Now everyone fell silent.

"Within our records are mysteries that must be solved. Powerful families who were once part of our order were allowed to drift away. Secrets and artifacts we swore to protect have been lost or forgotten. It will take the combined intellect and talents of all members to solve these mysteries.

"Therefore, starting now, all new trinities will be given a task, a puzzle to work, when they are called to the altar. Only when they've completed that task will they return to be formally married. Success or failure will impact their trinities, and their marriages."

There were exclamations of surprise, disgruntled mutterings from older members, and in the front, Harrison's eyebrows rose nearly to his hairline. The rumblings rose in volume, the situation seeming to slip out of the Grand Master's control.

Juliette held up her hand in a "stop" motion. Her will and authority flowed over the crowd. They fell silent and waited. Waited for orders from the Grand Master.

"This is not without danger. A box bearing our symbol and containing a secret message was left with a man who, two generations ago, was not called to the altar. His grandson wore his ring, not knowing the truth. The box, when opened, contained a deadly poison that nearly cost one of our members their life.

"A new trinity was tasked with solving this mystery. They uncovered past misdeeds and betrayals. We must right the wrongs of our past, ferret out threats to our society."

When she paused, there was a respectful silence.

"I will not allow disloyalty to our society or our mission. Together we will move forward, even as we respect and honor our past."

Juliette raised a glass. *"Mitimur in Vetitum."*

They repeated after her. *"Mitimur in Vetitum."*

We strive for the forbidden.

The Grand Master disappeared through an archway, Franco and Devon stepping out from behind the altar and going to mingle with the crowd, who quickly surrounded them in an effort to find out more about the new Grand Master. They answered the questions they could, and shook their heads when they were asked something they would not answer, such as who was the new Grand Master or what had happened to the previous one. No one would have dared asked if it had been a man's voice.

Juliette Adams slid into the room. She wore a sparkling white gown and a crystal broach in her hair. She snaked through the crowd, avoiding her friends. Because she'd grown up as a legacy, because she was known by many, it wouldn't take her friends long to figure out she was the new Grand Master. The great legacy families knew an Adams always had been, and always would be, the Grand Master.

Moving quickly, she found her brother in the crowd.

"Harrison."

He turned, his expression a combination of pride and alarm. "Juliette. Why don't we go and talk—"

"No. Thank you, but no. I appreciate your offer but I don't need your advice."

Harrison's jaw clenched, and then he nodded once. "Of course."

"But I do need something else. Will you stay after?"

He looked her over from head to foot, taking in the white gown and elegant hairdo. He smiled. "I'd be honored."

She took his hand and squeezed it before turning away.

"Juliette." Rose tapped her shoulder, pulling her attention.

"Rose." Juliette's heart lurched. Rose had been caught in the middle of her battle with Devon, and now that she and Devon were going to be part of a trinity, it was Rose who suffered the most.

So much had happened that Juliette hadn't considered what she would say if she saw Rose. She couldn't say much without revealing she was the one who'd broken the trinity.

It turned out she didn't need to say anything.

Rose hugged her, kissing her cheek. "You just answered most of my questions."

"Rose, I'm sorry. So sorry."

"Don't be. For the first time in my life, I don't know exactly what my future will be."

Juliette kissed Rose's cheek. "I hope it's a good feeling."

"It is. But, Juliette, don't give him too much of a hard time. He really does love you, even if he's an ass."

"He loves you, too."

"Not in the way he loves you. And not to be rude, but I love both of you as siblings more than anything." Rose kissed her cheek once more and squeezed her hands.

Juliette had mixed feelings as she watched the woman who would have been her wife walk away. But then she caught Franco's eye. He gifted her with a small secret smile.

She could do this. She was the Grand Master.

THIS ROOM WAS SMALL, an intimate space compared to the altar room. A few people had lingered though it was approaching dawn, so they'd decided to use the medallion room. The floor and walls were marble and a large bronze medallion with the Trinity Masters' symbol and logo was inlaid in the center of the floor. Three high-backed chairs faced the center of the room. They ignored the chairs. They were not three strangers called together to meet their trinity. They'd bypassed that ceremony.

Harrison Adams wore no robe, but when he spoke, his words carried the authority of the office he used to hold. "When you joined, you made a vow. You pledged your lives to our cause and our way. You've met your partners, your lovers, your spouses.

"You are here to be formally bound in the marriage of the Trinity Masters."

Juliette, Franco and Devon stepped forward. Harrison's voice was filled with emotion as he quietly officiated his sister's wedding. Like Harrison's own wedding, this was rushed—there'd been no bonding ceremony, and Franco had not gone through any of the new-member initiations or the six-month waiting period. But Juliette was the Grand Master and the only people who could have questioned her were her councilors, who were hardly going to raise objections. Besides, technically Franco was a legacy.

Juliette was radiant in her white dress, Franco and Devon both handsome in their tuxedos, though Devon looked tense. Only when they'd sealed their marriage with a kiss did Devon relax, prompting Franco to laugh.

Alexis and Michael appeared with one of the last bottles of Champagne, passing around flutes and toasting the new trinity.

When there was no one left but the three of them, Juliette sank to the floor, tracing the edges of the triquetra with her hand. Franco and Devon joined her.

"A lot of people know. They recognized my voice." Luckily

the shock over her being the Grand Master had prevented most people from asking what had happened and why Harrison wasn't the Grand Master.

"It doesn't matter. You're the Grand Master. Your word is law."

The tension that had built up over the past few days was finally dissipating. Her hands started to shake. "I'm not sure I can do this," she whispered.

They surrounded and comforted her. She had to be strong. Only they could see her fall apart.

"You can. It's in your blood."

"We won't let anyone hurt you."

Juliette Adams let them comfort her, let herself shake and cry in reaction to the stress of the evening. Then she rose, flanked by her new husbands, and went to celebrate her wedding night.

EPILOGUE

Sebastian should have been in Boston weeks ago. There were things happening there that he needed to deal with, things he needed to tell his best friend before she discovered them on her own.

Unfortunately, midway through his flight, he'd gotten word a shipment of arms he'd been tracking finally made its way to Libya. He'd had to make a split-second decision, and in the end he'd decided finding those guns was more important and had taken the next flight home. Locating and confiscating them had taken longer than he'd thought—weeks instead of days—and he'd had to ditch his phone along the way. He would have died if not for Anderson.

When he finally arrived in Boston, there was a letter waiting at the townhouse he co-owned with Juliette and a few friends. The expensive creamy paper was unmistakable. It was a letter from the Grand Master.

Sebastian,
You are called to the altar...

It was signed "Grand Master", but he knew that handwriting. He'd passed too many notes in high school English class with the author to not recognize that scribble as Juliette's.

Shit. This was bad. He needed to find Juliette and talk to her. She'd been his best friend since they were kids. Sebastian could only imagine how she must be feeling, knowing he'd lied to her for years. The dishonesty hadn't come easy to him, but he'd had no choice. Surely, she'd understand once he had a chance to explain.

Maybe.

He needed to touch base with his handler, Devon, and get a read on the situation. The Grand Master held absolute power over the Trinity Masters, and Sebastian was pretty sure that at the moment, the Grand Master was super-pissed at him.

That was exactly what he didn't need—his pissed-off best friend, who'd just found out that he was secretly a CIA asset, deciding who he should marry.

Juliette was good at revenge, and if he didn't find her soon, he might be facing a lifetime of it.

Are you ready for Sebastian's story? Elegant Seduction is available now. And be sure to download A Very Trinity Christmas, a free holiday short story, featuring the Grand Masters siblings, Harrison and Juliette. You can download it HERE.

Read the entire Trinity Masters: Secrets and Sin series.

    Hidden Devotion
    Elegant Seduction
    Secret Scandal
    Delicate Ties

Beloved Sacrifice
Masterful Truth

AND CHECK out these other series...all part of the Trinity Masters world.

FALL of the Grand Master
Elemental Pleasure
Primal Passion
Scorching Desire
Forbidden Legacy

MASTERS ADMIRALTY
Treachery's Devotion
Loyalty's Betrayal
Pleasure's Fury
Honor's Revenge
Bravery's Sin

THE HAYDEN BROTHERS
Fiery Surrender
Necessary Pursuit
Joyful Engagement (a novella)
Wrath's Storm

THE MAFIA
Suspicion's Fire

Desire's Addiction
Danger's Heir

WARRIOR SCHOLARS
Hollywood Lies

CALLING ALL FACEBOOK FANS! Did you know there's a group for fans of the Trinity Masters series? Come join Mari and Lila for behind-the-scenes stories, contests, exclusive sneak peeks, and hilarious text threads. Join the society right HERE.

CLICK to the next page to read the first chapter of Elegant Seduction.

ELEGANT SEDUCTION

 hapter One

Sebastian Stewart walked through the front doors of the Boston Public Library like a man with a noose around his neck. He had returned to the States at the ass crack of dawn that morning and headed straight to the legacy house, in hopes of catching Juliette there. He and his best friend—the new Grand Master—had some air to clear. A lot of it. He'd fucked up big time and had returned to Boston with the knowledge that he would have to work overtime to convince his oldest and dearest friend that he was truly sorry.

However, he hadn't found Juliette at the house the two of them shared with several other legacies of the Trinity Masters. Being raised as part of the elite, ultra-secret society came with some nice perks. One main bonus was the connections Sebastian had to very wealthy, successful members of society.

His family, like Juliette's, had been part of the Trinity Masters since the inception. Sebastian's parents, his two moms and his father, were high-ranking officials working in various areas of the Department of Justice. His biological mother was the head of the DOJ cybersecurity department, while his "Aunt Joyce" was a professor at Quantico. His dad was just recently named Deputy Director of the DEA after spending years in the field as one of the department's top agents.

When he considered his upbringing, he decided it shouldn't have come as any big shock to Juliette that he'd followed in his family's footsteps and pursued a career with the CIA.

However, it *was* a surprise. Because for the past few years, he'd lied to her, claimed he was employed as an aid worker. The lies hadn't rested easy on his shoulders, but he hadn't had a choice when it came to revealing the truth to her.

What he had found at the legacy house was a letter taped to the door of his bedroom. He hadn't spoken to Juliette and he hadn't told her he was coming home. Apparently it didn't matter. The Grand Master was keeping tabs on him. Sebastian had opened the letter, breaking the wax seal on the ornate envelope with a sinking feeling in the pit of his stomach.

The contents of the letter were the reason he was now dodging tourists in the front lobby of the public library, his head pounding due to lack of sleep, stress, and a healthy amount of pure fury.

She'd called him to the altar.

Juliette, in a pique of anger, had decided to punish him by setting him up with his trinity. He couldn't believe she was so furious with him that she'd seek revenge in such a petty, immature, *lifelong* way. And the worst part was she'd set up the ceremony knowing exactly what time his flight was landing, ensuring he wouldn't have time to talk to her beforehand.

He bypassed the library elevator and headed for the stairs. He needed to blow off some steam, to try to burn off some of this red-hot rage. When he reached the third floor, he made his way along the dingy aisle to the rare books room. Once inside the tiny room, he crossed to the storage closet door. As always, there was no one in the room. It was simple enough to enter the closet without being seen. He moved the book cart aside and pressed the secret button that revealed an ancient elevator.

Sebastian glanced at his watch and scowled. He was cutting it close. As it was, he'd barely have time to find the dressing room and don his robe before the bell rang to signal him into the chamber. Juliette had timed her revenge well.

The difference between the third floor of the library and the elegant hallway he found himself in when he stepped off the elevator never failed to feel like culture shock. Upstairs, the floors were covered in wall-to-wall carpeting that was thirty years past its prime, held to the floor with duct tape and dirt. In the Trinity Masters' chambers, the floors were pristine, sparkling granite that screamed of prestige, sophistication, power.

He walked down the corridor and took a deep, steadying breath as he approached the dressing rooms. He passed B and C before standing outside his own assigned room, A. Glancing at the closed doors, he could only assume that his future partners were ensconced inside, donning their own robes, waiting with nervous anticipation and the realization that their lives were about to change forever.

His temper flared hot once more. This was bullshit. No matter what lies he had told to Juliette in the past, everything he'd done had been to protect her, with the best interest of the Trinity Masters at heart.

The Trinity Masters protected the country—and they'd been doing so since his forefathers helped dump some tea into the harbor. To be a member of the Trinity Masters meant giving your life to the society and its cause. And if that meant you lied to your best friend about what you really did, then you lied. And if you had to hack your best friend's email on behalf of the U.S. government, then you hacked it.

In her heart, she knew that being a member meant getting your hands dirty, meant doing things that might seem unsavory, but were necessary. When they'd been teenagers she'd taken the high moral ground—a rebellion against her father, the Grand Master.

Now, Juliette *was* the Grand Master, had clearly found his file, and she was using her newfound power. For her to fuck with his life so carelessly was unforgivable.

He had returned to Boston to apologize. If Juliette went through with this, if she pledged his life to two strangers chosen specifically to punish him, then the apology would be hers to issue.

And he wouldn't accept it.

Sebastian entered the room, disappointed to find it empty save for the long black robe he was expected to wear to meet his assigned mates. Part of him—the optimistic part, the part who couldn't believe his best friend would do this to him—had hoped Juliette would be waiting in the room. That she'd punch him in the arm, call him a string of unsavory names, rant and rave for a bit, and then she'd tell him the rest had been a joke, a way to teach him a lesson for turning her into an unwitting CIA informant.

He looked in the mirror and studied the dark circles under his eyes. He'd spent thirty-two hours traveling from Tripoli to Boston with a long layover in Dubai. He had hoped to sleep on the plane, but stress had kept him awake, not allowing him to do more than doze for a few minutes at a time. He was exhausted and in the absolute worst frame of mind for what was about to come. Juliette used to chastise him for his short fuse, claiming he could go from zero to sixty quicker than anyone she'd ever met.

A bell sounded. Sebastian's chest constricted. He was supposed to undress. Members came to the altar in only their undergarments or some chose to wear nothing at all. Sebastian's father had once explained to him that part of the ceremony involved dropping the hood and discarding the robe. Bearing their bodies to each other symbolized that they were offering themselves completely, that they were coming to the union with nothing to hide.

Sebastian grabbed the black robe from the hanger and threw it on over his clothing. He didn't bother to remove his shoes. He wasn't okay with this. Wasn't okay with Juliette destroying his life as some petty act of vengeance.

He opened the door and stomped into the room. He hadn't lifted the hood to conceal his identity either. He was throwing all the traditions right back in Juliette's face.

Standing around the crest in the center of the room was a man and a woman. He could tell by the colors of their robes. The woman wore white and was a slight, tiny thing, while the man's build resembled that of an NFL linebacker, his long black robe barely reaching his feet.

Sebastian distinctly heard a gasp from the woman as he approached the circle. For a moment, he thought perhaps she was horrified by the fact he hadn't hidden his face. Then it occurred to him that perhaps her shock was based on recognition. He tried to peer beneath her hood, to sneak a peek at her, but the woman anticipated his actions and lowered her head.

Yep. She knew him. And given her response, she wasn't any happier about this union than he was. So there were two lives Juliette was fucking up. Sebastian turned his attention to the man standing directly across from him. He didn't attempt to hide his face. In fact, it seemed to Sebastian as if he was purposely letting the hood drift back, revealing his features. He was a stranger, no one Sebastian had ever seen before.

Which meant he wasn't a legacy. And he wasn't from Boston.

Sebastian had grown up surrounded by the Trinity Masters, born and bred at the heart of the secret society. He rooted for the Celtics, the Bruins, the Red Sox and the Patriots, and he'd spent years trying to drive the New England "ah"—found in pahty and pahking—out of his accent in order to perform his undercover duties with the agency.

Before he could study the man's features more closely, a side door opened and the Grand Master walked into the room in full regalia. They'd clearly had special robes made to fit Juliette. The long, rich velvet material was cut to accommodate her height and figure. If she'd attempted to wear her older brother Harrison's robes, they would have dragged several inches behind her.

It was hard for Sebastian to dredge up any of the sympathy he'd felt for his friend when she had learned Harrison had broken the rules of the Trinity Masters and was being forced to step down as Grand Master. Juliette had lived her life prior to that safe in the knowledge that her big brother would rule the society until his retirement or death, at which point any child he had would take over. When he had stepped down, childless, the leadership of the organization fell to her. She hadn't wanted it.

Sebastian had understood her reticence. It was a huge responsibility. Hundreds of members, political alliances, sociological, educational and scientific advances, and God only knew what else now rested on her shoulders.

But any compassion he felt for her situation had evaporated, boiled away to nothingness in the scorching rage coursing through him.

It was impossible to tell if Juliette was surprised to see his face so boldly revealed. Her face, like the woman's next to him, was well hidden beneath the hood of her robe.

When she began to speak, to say the words of the binding ceremony, Sebastian was once again shocked. That damn optimistic part of him was still waiting for her to call this farce off. The longer she spoke, the more he realized that wasn't going to happen. She had every intention of tying his future to these two people.

When it came time for introductions, she began with the other man.

"Grant Breton."

Sebastian had never heard of him, though there was something vaguely familiar about his last name.

Grant didn't hesitate to shed his robe. Beneath, he was completely naked. There was no shame or embarrassment. Sebastian's respect for the man rose.

Grant was an attractive man—clearly older than Sebastian—with dark-brown eyes and auburn hair. He had an air of confidence and a determined face that said he didn't put up with anyone's bullshit. It was a familiar look—one Sebastian saw in the mirror every morning.

When Juliette announced the other name, Sebastian understood just how deeply her anger toward him ran.

"Elyse Hunt."

Sebastian closed his eyes, unwilling to watch as Elyse removed her robe. When he didn't hear the swish of fabric hitting the floor, he opened them and realized she'd only lowered the hood. Her eyes were filled with apprehension and a bit of anger.

Juliette only paused a moment before saying his name. Like

Elyse, he refused to take off his robe. Though he couldn't see her face, he felt Juliette's gaze boring into him. Several long, painful moments passed as he tried to come to grips with everything he felt—anger, sorrow, frustration, disbelief. His gut ached, knowing that she would do this without a word, without giving him a chance to explain or apologize.

She was the best friend he'd ever had and her actions sliced through him like the sharpest knife, cutting deeply, painfully.

Finally, she released a quiet sigh, and then took the long gold chain that held the crest of the Trinity Masters from her neck. She bade them to each put a hand out, which they did. His was on the bottom. When Elyse hesitated too long, Grant placed his on top of Sebastian's, and Elyse placed hers on Grant's. The chain was looped around their stacked hands and Juliette completed the ceremony, said the last few words, each one forcibly striking the coffin she'd just nailed him inside.

No one spoke or made a move as silence permeated the air. Typically, the end of the ceremony—like that of a traditional wedding—included a kiss. That clearly wasn't going to happen here.

Juliette removed the chain and turned to leave the chamber. She was nearly to the door when Sebastian lost it. Before the door closed behind her, he caught it to follow Juliette and left his partners standing by the altar, their mouths agape.

Juliette spun angrily when she heard him following her down the small hallway that led to the Grand Master's office. These elegant chambers, buried deep beneath the Boston Public Library, were connected by a spider's web of secret passageways. He suspected no one truly knew where they all were or where they led to.

He opened his mouth to blast her, but she held up her hand.

"Wait," she commanded. "Just wait."

Then she continued toward her office, Sebastian in tow, being treated like a small child about to be chastised by the principal. That feeling didn't sit well with him.

She gestured to a chair in front of her large antique desk as she circled it to claim the space behind. She was purposely putting herself in the power seat, placing herself in the position of authority.

He didn't sit down.

"What the hell do you think you're doing?" Her voice was tight with anger.

Sebastian leaned toward her, looming, with his palms flat against the surface of her desk. "That's actually my question for you. Dammit, Juliette! This is my life you're playing with. I know you're pissed about the fact that I lied to you, but I can't believe you would—"

Juliette rose from the chair, placing her own hands against the desk. He had a foot on her, but when she leaned closer, fury flashing in her eyes, size ceased to matter. In this battle, they were equals, their rage burning at the same scorching level. "How dare you! Do you seriously think that I chose your trinity based on petty revenge? You're right, Bastian—" She all but spit the nickname he hated at him. "I am pissed. And hurt. You're my best friend and you lied to me and used me. For years."

Hearing her admit that he'd hurt her took some of the wind out of his sails. He loved her like a sister. Had since they were kids.

His lies were based on his desire to serve his country and the Trinity Masters. To keep America strong. She, of all people, should understand what that meant to him.

"Jules—" he started, his voice quieter as his anger began to fade.

Unfortunately, Juliette was just getting started. "Your behavior in there was appalling and it has me second-guessing my plan. It's clear I've made a horrible mistake. I thought you were the best man for this job, but now…"

Job? Plan? What the hell was she talking about?

"Jules—"

She was on a roll and unwilling to let him get a word in edgewise. God help her new husbands if they ever got into a lover's spat with her. It was impossible to win when she worked herself up into a lather.

She opened her mouth and looked as if she was about to start a truly epic rant—she was damn good at those—but no sound emerged. Instead, she paused and glanced around the room. She ran her hands over the surface of her desk. When she looked up, her face seemed older and there was a seriousness to her expression that seemed foreign.

With a start, Sebastian realized he wasn't just looking at his friend. This was the Grand Master.

"I needed your help, Seb."

And just like that, every bit of anger evaporated. He sat down.

"With what?"

Juliette looked at his face for thirty uncomfortable seconds. She was sizing him up, deciding if she wanted to carry out whatever plan it was that had driven her to unite him with a stranger and—shit—Elyse Hunt. He held her gaze, showed her that he was still the same man he'd always been. The one who would lay down his life for her.

When she slowly sank down into her seat, he saw shades of the same familiar Juliette reemerging. One side of her mouth tipped up in the lopsided grin she reserved for people she loved. Despite the smile, there were lines beside her eyes that were new, but that Sebastian suspected would be permanent. Becoming the Grand Master was no easy task and though she'd only assumed the position a few weeks ago, it was clearly taking its toll on her.

He hated to think she would never be the same carefree, fun-loving girl she'd been ever again. From now on, she would be this woman, more reserved, less likely to talk without thinking, more introspective...and suspicious.

Then he realized none of that mattered. She would always be his friend.

"You heard that I've selected my partners, joined a trinity?"

He nodded. He hadn't been surprised to hear she'd taken Devon as her husband; the two had been betrothed since they were kids. However, he had been shocked to discover she'd actually ended the planned union with the proposed third, Rose. Instead, Juliette had chosen a man Sebastian had never heard of as her other partner.

"I heard. What happened with Rose?"

Juliette's smile emerged more fully. "I'm the Grand Master now. And I figured I'd take advantage of some of the perks associated with it. I dissolved the original betrothal."

Sebastian frowned. "But you're still with Devon."

Suddenly Juliette's happy expression made more sense.

He grinned. "You finally admitted you were in love with him."

She lifted one shoulder noncommittally, but it wasn't as if his comment had been a question. He'd known for years how she felt about Devon, even if she couldn't admit it to herself.

It was clear she was genuinely pleased with her union. If he was a good friend, he'd be grateful for that. As it was, all he could think about was his own triad, the partners he'd left standing beside the altar as he stormed away from them.

"Once some of the dust settles around here, I want you to come have dinner with us and meet Franco. I think you'll really like him."

He appreciated the invitation—it gave him hope that all was going to be okay between them—but he couldn't get past the first part of her statement. "When what dust settles?"

"All is not as it seems with the Trinity Masters."

Well, that sounded ominous as fuck.

"What do you mean?"

Juliette pushed her chair closer to her desk and rested her elbows on top. "I think we've uncovered a secret sect."

"A secret sect in the secret society?" He spoke the words in jest. All his life, he'd had a hard time going to the movie theater to watch suspense thrillers. Primarily because he had always felt his life was far more exciting and interesting than the fictional variety. Hollywood couldn't hold a candle to the Trinity Masters.

She gave him a rueful grin that held no mirth. "Yeah. Certain documents have led me to believe we've lost some legacies, that there was a small faction of the group working in direct opposition to the beliefs the Trinity Masters always tried to uphold."

"In what way?"

"Apparently in the forties, there were some people who didn't like the direction the organization was taking. They didn't approve of the members being recruited, those the Trinity Masters felt had the strength and ability to fix all of society's ills. Poverty, education, workers' rights. Stuff like that."

"Why would they have issues with that?"

Juliette sighed. "Look at the time period. We'd come through the Great Depression, World War II was raging around us, Hitler had assumed scary amounts of power. It would be naïve of us to believe there weren't people living right here in America who didn't sympathize with the Nazi cause."

Sebastian wasn't sure how to reply. He'd grown up admiring and respecting the Trinity Masters. In his mind, it was this society that had kept the United States flourishing as a world power. And sure, maybe there was some naivety that came with that belief, but he'd lived his entire life surrounded by these people, by these incredible minds.

"Are you trying to tell me there were Nazis in the Trinity Masters?" It was a bit like finding out Santa Claus was the leader of ISIS. Sebastian couldn't quite wrap his head around it.

Juliette shook her head. "No. Nothing quite so specific. What we discovered was a small sect of purists, Trinity Masters with their own agenda, one that worked against the goals and purposes set forth by our founding fathers at the dawn of this country. The purists strongly believed we needed to keep our bloodlines more pure, limit the membership to only wealthy white people."

"This sounds like something straight out of Harry Potter."

Juliette rolled her eyes. "I wouldn't know."

He pursed his lips. "I gave you the whole damn set for Christmas and you still won't read it."

"Seb. Focus. Did you hear what I said?"

"I did. And I'm having a hard time believing it. That's one hell of a discovery to make."

"I know." Juliette stood and walked over to a bookshelf covered in dusty tomes that Sebastian would bet hadn't been touched in decades. After so many years, they'd simply become a part of the décor of the room.

Sebastian bent forward, resting his elbows on his knees and looking down at the expensive Oriental rug. He tended to see the world in black and white, good guys and bad guys. It was a characteristic that left him struggling more often than not in a world comprised solely of gray. In his mind, the Trinity Masters had always been black and white. He could count on them to do the right thing. "And you think these members were successful in their efforts?"

"I know they were. Franco was a lost legacy."

"You keep saying 'lost'. What does that mean?"

"His family was erased from our history books, allowed to disappear through the cracks via underhanded means."

Sebastian's brow creased in confusion, so Juliette tried to explain further. "His grandfather was never called to the altar, never allowed to continue. He was tricked into staying away."

"And you think there are others like him? Lost legacies?"

Juliette nodded. "I'm certain there are. And I'm determined to find them."

Juliette hadn't been happy when the leadership of the society was dumped onto her shoulders, but in that moment, Sebastian knew she'd be an incredible Grand Master. She was born to lead, but more than that, she had a huge heart, a tremendous need to correct injustices and make the world a better place.

"Good," he said. "They deserve to have their rightful place in the society."

"I knew you'd agree."

"Is that why I'm here? To help you find them?"

She shook her head. "No. Your task is slightly different. I need to know if the purists are still at work."

Sebastian reared back in his chair. "You think they're still functioning?"

She shrugged. "I don't know. Part of me thinks maybe they've always been there."

He blew out a long breath. While he appreciated the trust she was placing in him despite the revelations of the past few weeks, the pieces still weren't adding up.

"You know I'll help you any way I can, Jules. But I'm

confused about the triad. Why did you call me to the altar? You could have just told me what you needed done."

"Do you know the name Breton?"

Sebastian had recognized it, but he couldn't recall why. "It rings a bell, but no more than that."

"The only known purist we've been able to uncover is Jessica Breton, Grant's great-aunt. She was the member who tricked Franco's grandfather into staying away. Her means were lethal."

"And you want to see if this secret sect operates on the same legacy system the Trinity Masters use?"

"It's the only lead we have, Seb. I was hoping you could get close to Grant, feel him out, try to discover if he's a part of them. I decided the quickest and easiest way for you to accomplish that was to call you both to the altar together. You'll spend the next week together in the Presidential Suite at the Boston Park Plaza getting to know your partners, working out the details of setting up your lives together. I couldn't think of any other situation where you could get as close as you'd need to. You need access, a way to delve into his family's background, into his own personal values and beliefs without raising suspicions. Sex loosens tongues."

Jesus. She was right about intimacy lowering walls and inviting confidences, but Sebastian wasn't sure how he felt about crawling into bed with the guy to discover his secrets. He wanted to help, but he was straight. And Juliette knew that.

"That may all be true, but that's a hell of a sacrifice you've just asked me to make. Essentially, you've tied me to the man for the rest of my life simply to spy on him."

Juliette walked over to him and placed her hand on his shoulder. "The true binding ceremony, the permanent marriage, doesn't happen for thirty days. As Grand Master, I hold the power to dissolve unions during this trial period. I can't break up a triad once it's made truly official, but I can at any time during the next month."

"It's not forever?"

Juliette shook her head. "No. I don't intend for this to be your true trinity, but it also doesn't give you much time."

Thirty days. He only had thirty days to uncover one hell of a secret. And given his actions at the altar, he would probably have to spend every minute of that time simply getting his "pretend" partners to speak to him again.

"I'll do it, but I'm afraid I may have already shot myself in the foot with the way I behaved back there."

Juliette's eyes narrowed and her spine stiffened.

Nice job, Seb. Way to remind her you were the world's biggest jackass.

She lifted her finger and a shiver ran through him. Sebastian had never been afraid of Juliette, but her intimidating stance reminded him once more that she was not the girl he used to know. "By the way, if you ever treat me—the Grand Master—with that level of disrespect again, I won't hesitate to go all Queen of Hearts on your ass."

Sebastian smiled, rose and placed his hand over his chest as he made a vow. "I'm extremely sorry for my behavior, Grand Master."

She appeared only slightly appeased, so he reached out to take her hand.

"Jules, if I'm ever so thick-skulled as to doubt our friendship again, I'll walk to the guillotine and put my own head on the chopping block."

She laughed softly and they hugged. For the first time since landing in Boston this morning, Sebastian was able to take a deep breath.

As they stayed there, letting all the bad feelings drop away, Sebastian realized there was still a question left unanswered.

"There's one more thing I don't understand. Where does Elle Hunt figure into this union?"

Juliette stepped out of his grasp, her face radiating pure evil delight. "Oh, *she* was your punishment for lying to me all these years."

CONTINUE READING! Elegant Seduction is available now.

ABOUT THE AUTHORS

Virginia native Mari Carr is a *New York Times* and *USA TODAY* bestseller of contemporary sexy romance novels. With over two million copies of her books sold, Mari was the winner of the Romance Writers of America's Passionate Plume for her novella, *Erotic Research*.

Join her newsletter so you don't miss new releases and for exclusive subscriber-only content. You can visit Mari's website at https://maricarr.com or email her at mari@maricarr.com.

Lila Dubois is an award winning author of erotic, paranormal and fantasy romance. Her book J is for..., the tenth book in the bestselling checklist series, won the 2019 National Readers' Choice Award. Additionally, she's been nominated for the RT Book Reviews Erotic Novella of the Year for Undone Rebel and the Golden Flogger.

Having spent extensive time in France, Egypt, Turkey, Ireland and England Lila speaks five languages, none of them (including English) fluently. Lila lives in California with her own Irish Farm Boy and loves receiving email from readers.

You can visit Lila's website at www.liladubois.net. She loves to hear from fans! Send an email to author@liladubois.net or join her newsletter.

Made in the USA
Las Vegas, NV
21 January 2026

39872969R00125